LP CRI
Crider, Bill.
Red, White & Blue murder.

DATE DUE

AP1
AP2

D

RED,
WHITE,
AND BLUE
MURDER

Also by Bill Crider
in Large Print:

A Time for Hanging
Galveston Gunman
Medicine Show
Ryan Rides Back

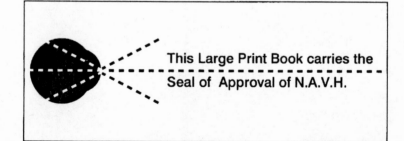

RED,
WHITE,
AND BLUE
MURDER

A Sheriff Dan Rhodes Mystery

BILL CRIDER

WHEELER
PUBLISHING

Published in 2004 by arrangement with St. Martin's Press, LLC.

Wheeler Large Print Compass.

The text of this Large Print edition is unabridged.
Other aspects of the book may vary from the original edition.

Set in 16 pt. Plantin by Christina S. Huff.

Printed in the United States on permanent paper.

Library of Congress Cataloging-in-Publication Data

Crider, Bill, 1941–
    Red, white, and blue murder : a sheriff Dan Rhodes mystery /
Bill Crider.
        p.   cm.
    ISBN 1-58724-555-8 (lg. print : hc : alk. paper)
    1. Rhodes, Dan (Fictitious character) — Fiction.   2. Fourth of
July — Fiction.   3. Sheriffs — Fiction.   4. Texas — Fiction.
5. Large type books.   I. Title.
PS3553.R497R43 2004
813′.54—dc22   2003065783

For Jeff Meyerson,
who won't have to ask where I get my ideas

As the Founder/CEO of NAVH, the only national health agency solely devoted to those who, although not totally blind, have an eye disease which could lead to serious visual impairment, I am pleased to recognize Thorndike Press★ as one of the leading publishers in the large print field.

Founded in 1954 in San Francisco to prepare large print textbooks for partially seeing children, NAVH became the pioneer and standard setting agency in the preparation of large type.

Today, those publishers who meet our standards carry the prestigious "Seal of Approval" indicating high quality large print. We are delighted that Thorndike Press is one of the publishers whose titles meet these standards. We are also pleased to recognize the significant contribution Thorndike Press is making in this important and growing field.

Lorraine H. Marchi, L.H.D.
Founder/CEO
NAVH

★ Thorndike Press encompasses the following imprints: Thorndike, Wheeler, Walker and Large Print Press.

1

If he stood out in his backyard just after sunup, Sheriff Dan Rhodes could almost make himself believe that the whole day would be as cool and pleasant as that brief moment in the early morning.

But he knew better. The sky was turning blue, and there were a few feathery clouds that looked as if someone had colored them with a pink crayon, but the clouds would be gone before long. The air was so dry that there was no dew on the grass, and by noon the sun would have boiled the sky to blazing incandescence.

It was the second of July. There hadn't been any rain to speak of in Blacklin County in nearly two months, and before that, hardly any rain for nearly three years. In fact, the last good rain Rhodes could remember had been during the writers' workshop out at the old college in Obert, and that had been quite a while ago.

The ground beneath the scorched brown grass in Rhodes's yard had two-inch cracks in it, and all around the town of Clearview, the stock tanks were drying up. There was no grass for the cattle to graze on, nothing but needle grass and weeds. Even most of the johnsongrass in the bar

7

ditches had dried to a crackly brown. The ranchers were despairing of having any hay for the winter.

There was one good thing that had come from the weather, however, at least as far as Rhodes was concerned. He hadn't had to mow his yard in weeks. The town hadn't yet put restrictions on water use, but he didn't think it would be right to water his yard when the situation was becoming critical. Besides, he hated mowing.

Speedo, Rhodes's outside dog, tried to keep up appearances by pretending to be interested in the ball that Rhodes threw for him to fetch, but Rhodes could tell that the dog's heart wasn't really in it. He wasn't moving half as fast as he did on cool fall days, and instead of hanging on to the ball and making Rhodes wrest it from between his teeth, he dropped it at Rhodes's feet and wandered off, as if already looking for a nice shady spot to spend the day.

Rhodes knew the spot Speedo was thinking about. It was under a pecan tree, where the dog had worn the thin covering of grass away and gotten to the cool dirt beneath. The leaves on the tree looked shriveled, and if it gave up any pecans in the fall, they would be few and small because of the lack of water.

Yancey, Rhodes's inside dog, who had been released for the moment to romp around the yard, didn't show much enthusiasm either. Yancey was a Pomeranian, and he spent most of his time in the house either yapping, yipping, or

8

sleeping. When he came into the yard, he yapped constantly and chased Speedo from one corner to the other, looking a lot like a bouncing Q-Tip as he harassed the much larger dog. Today, he looked more like a slowly rolling dust bunny. He was still yapping, but Speedo was ignoring him, and Yancey didn't really seem to care.

"I have some good news for you, fellas," Rhodes said to the dogs. "No fireworks for the Fourth this year."

He didn't know how Yancey felt about fireworks, but Speedo didn't like the explosions. He usually spent the evening in his Styrofoam igloo. But this year he didn't have to worry. The danger of fire was too great, and the annual fireworks show at the Clearview City Park had been canceled.

In the past, Rhodes had been much more fond of explosions than Speedo. He still liked them but recent events had changed his point of view. He'd nearly been blown up twice, and the experiences had tended to sour him on explosions. Nevertheless, he was more or less expected to show up at the big Fourth of July celebration, though he could have seen the fireworks, if there had been any, almost as well from his house as he could in the park. But he always attended, and he'd be there again this year.

Even without the fireworks, there would be other festivities, like the barbecue cook-off and the historical pageant, though the heat would be brutal. People assumed that the county sheriff would be there, and Rhodes would have to put in an appearance. He thought he'd rather curl up under the pecan tree with Speedo, though he did like barbecue with spicy sauce, even in the summer.

Rhodes heard the screen door slam behind him and turned to see his wife, Ivy, standing on the little back porch. She had short gray hair and a trim figure that Rhodes admired a great deal.

Apparently Yancey admired it too, or admired something about her. He perked up, bounced over, and started yipping around her ankles. Like Speedo, Ivy ignored him.

"Hot enough for you?" she asked Rhodes.

Rhodes gave her a thoughtful look.

"If I had my pistol, I'd shoot you for saying that," he told her.

"I thought it was pretty clever."

"So does everybody else in the county. Do you know how many times a day I hear that line?"

"Two?" Ivy said. "Three?"

"Three hundred is more like it. There should be a law against it."

"Well," Ivy said, "there's one good thing —"

"Don't say it."

"— it's a dry heat," Ivy finished.

"I'm going for the pistol now. No jury in the world would convict me."

"You can't shoot me," Ivy said. "I can say anything I want to. This is America. Freedom of speech and all that. The freedom doesn't extend to shooting people, though. Besides, wife-shooting wouldn't look good on your record when you have to run again, even if you weren't convicted."

"I think the voters would understand."

"The voters are the ones who're asking if it's hot enough for you," Ivy said.

Rhodes admitted that she might have a point.

"I know I do. Do you think there'll be any fires today?"

Rhodes hoped not. There had already been too many, mostly little ones, grass fires that were easily put out, but he was worried that sooner or later there might be a real conflagration. Maybe on the Fourth of July.

"It's too bad we don't have a law against fire-works," he said.

"I thought we did."

"Clearview does. The city can pass ordi-nances like that. The county government can't. So once you're out of the city limits, you can sell fireworks, you can set them off, you can do pretty much what you want to. Grat Bilson's been trying to get something done about it in the county for years, but he hasn't had any luck."

Yancey continued to yip and yap and dance around Ivy's ankles. She pushed him aside with her foot, but he didn't mind. He moved right back in.

"I thought you liked fireworks," Ivy said to Rhodes.

"I do," Rhodes said. "But I think they should be handled by a licensed pyro. Otherwise, they're dangerous, especially in weather like this. One Roman candle ball that gets into a bunch of dry johnsongrass, and a whole pasture can go up."

"I didn't think there was enough grass to burn."

"Sure there is. On places where there aren't any cattle, there's grass. And sometimes a house. Not to mention a little woods. It can be pretty bad."

"Why doesn't the state do something?" Ivy asked.

"I don't really know. But there's a lot of money to be made off fireworks."

"You don't think the legislators are being bribed, do you?"

"No. They probably get some big campaign contributions, though. Anyway, there are plenty of other things that can cause fires. I was just thinking about fireworks because it's so close to the Fourth."

Ivy reached down and picked up Yancey. He wriggled with pleasure, but he didn't stop his yipping.

"Maybe we could tie your little dog here to a bottle rocket and send him to the moon," Ivy said.

"*My* dog? I thought he was *our* dog."

"You're the one who brought him home."

That was true. Rhodes had found both Speedo and Yancey in the course of his investigations, and he hadn't wanted to leave them without someone to take care of them. So he'd brought them home.

"But you love him," Rhodes said. "Anyway, cruelty to animals is worse than shooting people. Especially who ask if it's hot enough for me."

Ivy set Yancey down. Instead of assaulting her ankles, he went to the door and yapped.

"I think he's had enough of the great outdoors," Rhodes said. "I don't blame him."

Ivy opened the door, and Yancey ran inside, his little claws clicking on the hardwood floor. Rhodes went to check on Speedo's water bowl. It was about half full, but Rhodes dumped the water out and refilled the bowl.

"Do you think the historical societies will get along this year?" Ivy asked when Rhodes had finished with the water bowl.

Blacklin County had two historical societies, the Clearview Historical Association and the Sons and Daughters of Texas. While it seemed to Rhodes that they both had similar goals, the members of one group never seemed able to agree with the members of the other on how to reach them. Not so long ago, the presidents of both associations had been murdered, and there had been a lot of talk about the two groups consolidating. But it hadn't happened.

"You never can tell what they'll do," Rhodes said. "Now that Grat Bilson's taken over as president of the Sons and Daughters and Vernell Lindsey's president of the Association, things are more unstable than they ever were."

Both Vernell and Bilson had had dealings with Rhodes in the past. Bilson was a combative man who had a contentious relationship with his wife, Yvonne. Vernell was Clearview's celebrity, the author of several romance novels published under the name Ashley Leigh.

"The fireworks were always the biggest problem," Ivy said. "Maybe everything will go off perfectly this year."

"We'll see," Rhodes said, not believing it for a minute.

2

The day went downhill from that point on. By the time Rhodes arrived at the jail, the temperature was already hitting ninety. He was glad to get into the air-conditioned office.

"Hot enough for you?" Hack Jensen, the dispatcher, asked when Rhodes came through the door, barely beating Lawton, the jailer, to the question.

Rhodes thought about shooting both of them, but, as Ivy had mentioned, it wouldn't look good on his record. A sheriff shouldn't go around shooting county employees. People might take it amiss.

"It could be worse," Lawton said with a sly look. "At least it's a dry heat."

"I'm going to lock both of you up if I hear you say that stuff again," Rhodes told them.

"Lock us up, and we'll just become a party to the lawsuit," Hack said.

"Lawsuit? Which lawsuit?"

"The one the prisoners'll be filin'," Hack said. "They claim it's too hot in the cell block, which is cruel and unusual. They've been complainin' for the last week."

"To me," Lawton said. "Not to him."

It seemed to Rhodes that Lawton and Hack were in constant competition, each one trying to one-up the other. They were both long past the usual retirement age, but they were also so good at their jobs that no one had suggested they quit, least of all Rhodes, who was willing to put up with a lot from someone who knew his job.

"Hack don't know a thing about it," Lawton went on. "He sits in here and watches his little TV and plays on that computer that belongs to the county, but I'm the one who has to deal with those prisoners every single day. I'm the one who has to get up close and personal with 'em. I'm the one —"

"Yeah, yeah, yeah," Hack said. "We know all about it. But I'm the one who has to take the phone calls and deal with Mr. and Mrs. John Q. Public. Ms. J.Q., too. I'm the one who takes all the abuse from the taxpayers when the high sheriff don't do things to satisfy 'em. I'm the one —"

"All right," Rhodes said, holding up a hand. "I know how much the two of you have to suffer. I'll hit the commissioners up for a raise at the next meeting."

"No you won't," Hack said. "You're just tellin' us that to get us to shut up."

"I'm telling you that because I want to hear about the lawsuit. Or have you forgotten about that?"

"Nobody's forgot," Hack said.

"Good. Now who's going to tell me about it?"

"Let Hack tell you," Lawton said. "Since he knows so much about it."

"All I know is that the prisoners say they're goin' to file one."

"And he only knows that 'cause I told him," Lawton said. "It's that Andy Tobin again, Sheriff."

Tobin, who had a serious drinking problem, was a frequent resident of the Blacklin County Jail. He was generally a troublemaker when he was there, and he was the one who, during his last visit, had filed a grievance because he claimed that the jailhouse was haunted.

"Maybe you should sic the ghost on him again," Hack suggested to Rhodes.

Rhodes said he thought that was a bad idea. It would just get the prisoners all worked up.

"They're already worked up," Lawton said. "Tobin's looking in the law books, and it won't be long before they file that suit. You can mark my words."

"It won't be the first time we've been sued," Hack said. "We ain't lost yet."

"We'll just see what happens," Rhodes said. "Maybe it will rain soon and cool things off."

"Nope," Hack said. "That weather guy on Channel Eight says it won't rain for the next five days at least, and maybe not for the five after that. There's this big dome of high pressure sittin' on top of us. That's like a mountain of air, he says, and there's nothing to move it. Best we can hope for is that a hurricane'll form out in the Gulf and come onto shore down around Houston. That'd move it."

"Wouldn't be too good for those folks down on the coast, though, would it?" Lawton said.

"That's their lookout," Hack said.

"That's just like you," Lawton said. "Always thinkin' of yourself."

Hack started to stand up, and Rhodes thought he might have to separate them, but he was saved by the ringing of the telephone.

Hack answered, listened, and then said, "There's a reporter wants to talk to you, Sheriff."

There was only one reporter who would be calling, Rhodes thought, and that was Jennifer Loam, who had come to Clearview to work for the *Herald* the previous fall. It was her first job after graduating from college. She was young, intense, and hoping to make some kind of name for herself so she could move on to a bigger paper in a bigger town.

"I'll take it at my desk," Rhodes said.

He sat down, picked up his phone, and punched the button that let him pick up the call.

"This is Sheriff Rhodes," he said.

"This is Jennifer Loam, of the Clearview *Herald*," the reporter said, as if Rhodes didn't know her and as if there might be another paper in town, which there wasn't. There wasn't another paper in the whole county.

18

But Rhodes didn't see any need to point those things out. He said, "What can I do for you, Ms. Loam?"

"There's something I have to discuss with you, Sheriff. Privately."

Rhodes looked over his shoulder. Lawton and Hack were listening to every word, just as they always did.

"This is pretty private," Rhodes said. "What do we have to discuss?"

"It isn't something I want to talk about on the phone. Can we meet?"

"Come on over. I'll be here for a while."

"I meant meet privately. Somewhere that there won't be anyone listening in."

"Sounds pretty serious," Rhodes said.

"It is."

"Can you give me a hint?"

Jennifer made a small sound that might have been either disgust or frustration. She said, "I don't suppose you're aware that I've been working on an exposé on some of the county commissioners."

Uh-oh, Rhodes thought. Suddenly the airconditioning didn't seem to be working so well.

"You're right," he said. "I wasn't aware of that."

"I have a . . . source who's come up with a lot of damaging information."

The four commissioners, along with the county judge, were the governing body for Blacklin County. That's the way it was all over the state, for that matter. It didn't make any difference whether you lived in a county with millions of people or a county with hundreds. There were still four commissioners and a judge. They controlled the county budget and made decisions about libraries, law enforcement, and road construction, among other things.

"I can see why you don't want to talk about it on the phone," Rhodes said.

"Oh, that's not the reason. I don't mind talking about the commissioners on the phone."

"Then what's the problem?"

"My informant has come up with some information about another county official."

"And who would that be?"

"That would be you, Sheriff."

"Oh," Rhodes said. "Maybe we'd better meet privately."

"I thought you might see it that way," Jennifer said.

3

They met in Rhodes's office in the county courthouse, which was located near the jail. Rhodes hardly ever went there, since he preferred working out of the jail, but he dropped in now and then when he needed some privacy or some time to think.

He walked from the jail, and he hadn't gone more than ten yards before he'd begun sweating. He was glad to get under the shade of the pecan trees that surrounded the courthouse, and gladder still to get inside the old building, which, with its high ceilings and marble floors, seemed to be even cooler than it actually was.

Another nice thing about the building was the Dr Pepper machine on the second floor not far from Rhodes's office, where you could still get Dr Pepper in glass bottles. Rhodes wasn't sure who was responsible for the machine, but he suspected that Jack Parry, the county judge, had some kind of arrangement with the local bottler.

For about a second, Rhodes wondered if that was the scandal that Jennifer Loam had uncovered about the commissioners.

Couldn't be, he thought. Who'd care about a thing like that?

He put his money in the coin slot. There was a rattling inside the machine, and Rhodes was rewarded with a chilled glass bottle that slid out of the chute. He opened it and took a drink. It felt cold all the way down his throat, and he hoped that Jennifer Loam wasn't going to deprive him of one of life's little pleasures by having the machine taken away.

There was no one in the office. Rhodes didn't even keep a secretary there. The telephone was forwarded to the jail, so if anyone called, Hack would answer and pass the word to Rhodes.

Rhodes sat behind his desk, which needed dusting, and waited for the reporter. As he drank his Dr Pepper, he wondered what Jennifer Loam's informant could possibly have said about him. As far as he knew, he hadn't done anything wrong.

He hoped her big story wasn't something about the money the county was wasting on maintaining an office for him when he spent hardly any time there. He thought the expense was justifiable, but it was possible not everyone would see it that way.

In about ten minutes, Jennifer Loam knocked on the pebbled glass of the door. She didn't wait for an answer, just opened the door and came in. She looked very young to Rhodes, but then he was finding that more and more people were looking young to him these days. He stood up and said, "Hot enough for you?"

Jennifer looked at him for a second and then laughed.

"I'm never sure what to make of you, Sheriff," she said. "But somehow I think you know you're the fifth person today who's asked me that." She glanced at her watch, a sensible Timex. "And it's not even nine o'clock."

"I was hoping to impress you with my wit," Rhodes said. "Why don't we sit down."

He sat behind the desk, and Jennifer sat in a dusty leather-covered chair across from him.

"Now tell me about this scandal you've uncovered," Rhodes said.

"This isn't funny," Jennifer told him. "I'm very serious about it."

Rhodes didn't doubt it. He said, "I'm not joking. I'd really like to know. If you've uncovered something about me, I'm glad you're going to talk to me before you publish something in the paper. Have you talked to the commissioners yet?"

"I tried."

Rhodes asked what she meant.

"They were very condescending. Insulting. One of them called me 'little lady' and told me a blonde joke."

"Which one?"

"Jay Beaman. He asked me if I was going to do a story about how you could fry an egg on the sidewalk."

Rhodes had actually seen stories like that in the Clearview *Herald*. Once, though, someone

23

had tried to fry the egg on the hood of a car.

"I'm sure Mr. Beaman didn't mean anything by that," Rhodes said.

"Ha. They all think I'm just some dumb kid just out of college."

"You're not dumb," Rhodes said. He decided he wouldn't bother to point out that she *was* just out of college.

"I know I'm not dumb. But they don't. They treat me like I was their daughter or something. I'm surprised I didn't get a pat on the head. They'll be sorry, though."

"I guess I'll be sorry, too, if you have something on me."

"I hate that part of it," Jennifer said. "You've always treated me like an adult, and you seem like an honest man. I liked the way you handled that kidnaping."

At Christmas, Jennifer had gotten her first big story when someone took the baby Jesus from the town's living manger scene.

"It wasn't exactly a real kidnaping," Rhodes said.

"There was a real murder, though, and you solved that."

"Just doing my job," Rhodes said, wishing he had a forelock to tug.

A few years ago, he'd had a forelock, but lately he'd noticed that his hair seemed to be getting a bit thinner in front. In the back, too, for that matter.

"And you do your job very well," Jennifer

said. "I find it pretty hard to believe that you'd do anything illegal."

"Thanks," Rhodes said. "I'm glad you have confidence in me. Just what illegal act is it that I'm supposed to have performed, by the way?"

Jennifer sat up a bit straighter and said primly, "I'm sure you know."

"Just for the purpose of discussion, let's pretend that I don't."

"I'm the one who should be asking the questions. You're just trying to find out how much I know."

"No," Rhodes said. "I'm not. I honestly can't think of a thing. I need your help here. After all, you're the one who called."

Jennifer considered that. She must have decided that Rhodes had a point because she said, "I guess I was hoping you'd confess. But since you're not going to, I'll tell you. After all, you're innocent until proven guilty in a court of law."

"That's good to know. And I might not be proven guilty even in a court of law if I haven't done anything illegal."

"Right. But you did. You had county inmates paint your house."

Rhodes didn't know what he'd expected to hear, but that hadn't been it. He said, "No, I didn't."

"Oh, I don't blame you for denying it. But my source says that you did. He has the photographs to prove it. And it gets worse. You used

25

one of your deputies to supervise the inmates while they were out of the jail."

"I hate to disillusion you," Rhodes said, "but sometimes people have it in for the sheriff. They might think he's not doing a good job, or they might not like having been picked up for DWI after some party they went to, or they might not like it that their son or daughter got stopped for speeding. So they might decide to get even by calling a reporter and lying to her about him. That's probably what it is in this case."

"You sound almost like you mean that," Jennifer said, looking a little surprised.

Rhodes was disappointed in the surprise. He'd more or less expected that she would believe him unhesitatingly. He should have known better, however, because it was true that he'd recently had his house painted. He could see how that might look bad to her. But he would never use inmates for a job like that. And he would certainly never have used a deputy to supervise. The deputies had enough to do without that kind of thing being added to their duties.

"Roy Dean Turner painted my house," he said. "I have the receipts for the labor and for the paint. I'll be glad to show them to you. And you can ask my neighbors if there were ever any inmates around the place. They'll tell you there weren't. Inmates are pretty easy to spot in those orange jumpsuits they wear, and my neighbors are the kind of people who'd notice."

"And you have the receipts?"

"Sure. I always save receipts. You can ask Roy Dean, too. He put a little sign up in the yard while he was working there: THIS HOUSE BEING PAINTED BY ROY DEAN TURNER. I DO THE JOBS YOUR HONEY DON'T DO. CALL FOR AN ESTIMATE. He did good work, and he might even have gotten another job or two because of the sign."

"But that can't be right. Are you sure there were no inmates involved?"

"You don't have to take my word for it. Ask Roy Dean. Ask my wife. Ask my neighbors. Let me show you the receipts."

Jennifer looked genuinely puzzled.

"Why would my source lie to me?" she said.

Rhodes had an idea about that. He said, "Maybe he was lying to you about the commissioners, too. People get upset with them, the same way they get upset with me. Maybe the ditches haven't been mowed, or maybe the roads in front of their houses haven't been graded in a while. Little things like that irritate some people, and they want to cause trouble for whoever's supposedly responsible."

"He wasn't lying. He wouldn't do that."

There was a hint of doubt in Jennifer's voice, and Rhodes could tell she was disappointed. Obviously the story meant a lot to her.

"He lied about me, didn't he?" Rhodes said. "Maybe that's why the commissioners treated you the way they did."

27

Jennifer didn't let him get away with his half-hearted defense.

"Ha," she said. "They treated me that way because they think no one cares about what they do. They get together and vote, and no one ever questions them. How many members of the public ever attend a commissioners' meeting? None, that's how many."

Rhodes remembered at least once when there had been quite a few people present at a meeting, but that was before Jennifer had come to town. Besides, she had a point. Most of the time, no one was there other than the commissioners themselves, and Rhodes if he had the chance.

"All one of those men — and they're all men, you notice. How many counties have women on the commissioners court?"

Rhodes said that he didn't know.

"Probably none. I'll do a little research and find out before I start my series of articles. Anyway, I was about to say that it's all buddy-buddy and good-old-boying. All one of those men has to do to get the votes he needs for any project at all is talk to two of his pals and promise he'll support them the next time some pet scheme of theirs comes up. They trade votes like little boys swapping baseball cards."

"That may be true," Rhodes said, "but it's not illegal."

"That's not what I'm writing about, either. It just makes me angry."

"What *are* you writing about, then?"

"You'll see. I can't understand why my source would try to implicate you in something, though, especially since it would be so easy to prove he was wrong. You *can* prove it, right?"

"I can prove it," Rhodes said, though he was sorry that he had to. "I'll bring the receipts to the jail, and you can stop by and see them any time. Feel free to call Roy Dean Turner and Ivy, too."

"I will," Jennifer said.

"Are you going to mention this in your story?"

"Mention what?"

"That your source lied about me. It might have some bearing on the way your readers think about the rest of your story."

Jennifer wasn't slow. She caught on at once.

"You mean they might doubt me," she said, "but that I should give them all the evidence. And you're right, so I'll mention it. But it won't make any difference. I have plenty of evidence about the commissioners."

"Which ones?" Rhodes asked.

Jennifer smiled. "That was pretty sneaky, Sheriff. But it won't work. You'll have to read about it in the *Herald* like everyone else."

"What kind of evidence do you have?"

"You'll have to read about that, too."

"It'll have to be good," Rhodes said.

"Why?"

"Because no one will believe you if it's not.

Your source lied about one thing. Why wouldn't he lie about the rest?"

"That could be a problem, I guess."

"And who did you say your source was?"

"I didn't say, and you won't find the answer in the paper, either. Reporters never reveal their sources. It's like Watergate. Nobody knows who Deep Throat was, not even after all this time."

Rhodes was pretty sure that Jennifer hadn't even been born during the Watergate mess, so she must have learned about it in college. It was nice to know that she'd paid attention in her classes.

"I won't press you," Rhodes said, "and I appreciate your coming to talk to me before printing anything about that house painting. I don't know where a story like that could have come from."

"I'll see if I can find out," Jennifer told him.

"If you do," Rhodes said, "give me a call. I'd like to know."

"I can't tell you if it would compromise my source."

"I understand, but let me know whatever you can."

Jennifer stood up and pushed back her chair.

"I'll do that. Maybe I'll have something to tell you when I come by to look at the receipts. Probably tomorrow."

Rhodes stood up as well.

"I'll see you tomorrow, then," Rhodes said.

"Count on it," Jennifer told him.

"If I'm not there, I'll leave the receipts in my desk. Hack will know where they are."

"That's fine. I'm going to call Mr. Turner, too, you know."

"I didn't doubt it for a second," Rhodes said.

4

After the young reporter had left, Rhodes sat back down behind his desk and thought things over, wondering just exactly what was going on. He supposed it wouldn't be too surprising if one of the commissioners, or even a couple of them, had gotten involved in a little bit of hanky-panky. It happened from time to time, all over the state.

The trouble was that Rhodes knew the commissioners, worked with them, and for the most part respected them. He'd known one of them, James Allen, ever since he was young. They'd played football together in high school, even dated a few of the same girls. Rhodes hoped that if anyone was actually guilty of wrongdoing, it wouldn't be Allen.

But maybe it wasn't anyone at all. It was easy to make accusations, but it was a lot harder to prove them. That business about the house painting, for example. How could anyone have expected to prove that he'd used inmates on that job? It didn't make any sense at all.

It was true that from time to time there would be articles in the paper about other sheriffs using inmates for personal work, like mowing the sheriff's lawn or plowing up his garden in the spring, but Rhodes had never even considered doing anything like that. Though come to think of it, being allowed to use inmates for mowing his lawn would have been an excellent fringe benefit, at least in the years when there was enough rain for the grass to grow.

But the story about the house painting was simply ridiculous. Probably half the town had seen Turner's sign in Rhodes's front yard, and they'd also seen Turner himself, or one of his helpers, climbing around on a low scaffold or ladder, painting the eaves and soffit boards. Rhodes hadn't wanted a spray-paint job, so the work had taken several days to complete.

He wished that Jennifer had given him a hint about what she was going to charge the commissioners with. Of course he could always go talk to James Allen and find out what he knew. Allen had proved helpful more than once in the past.

Rhodes picked up the dusty telephone and called Hack to let him know where he'd be.

"You goin' by to give Miz Wilkie a thrill?" Hack asked.

Mrs. Wilkie was a woman who had once set her cap for Rhodes, in the days when Rhodes had been single. She'd thought Rhodes would make an excellent replacement for her dead husband. After Rhodes had married Ivy, Mrs. Wilkie had taken a job as James Allen's secretary.

"I don't think anything I do would thrill Mrs. Wilkie," Rhodes said.

Hack laughed. "You know better'n that. She'd marry you in a New York minute if you'd just see the light and get rid of Ivy. Look at how she's changed since you got married."

"The only thing that's changed about her is her hair," Rhodes said.

After her plans for Rhodes had fallen through, Mrs. Wilkie had allowed her hair, which had been dyed a bizarre shade of orange, to return to its natural color, which was mostly gray.

"She took that job, too," Hack said. "That was a mighty big change for her."

"So?"

"So she's provin' to you that she can fend for herself, just like Ivy can."

Rhodes suspected that Hack was onto something, not that it mattered. He liked Mrs. Wilkie, but he'd never been interested in marrying her.

"Maybe you're right," he told Hack, "but she doesn't have to prove anything to me. It's too late for anything like that."

"It's never too late," Hack said. "Soon as you realize what a fine woman Miz Wilkie is, you'll divorce Ivy and marry her. It could happen."

"I don't think so. Give me a call if anything comes up."

"Don't I always?"

"Yes," Rhodes said. "You do."

Rhodes walked back to the jail and got the county car. The inside was like the inside of a brick pizza oven. Rhodes opened the windows to let some of the hot air out, but the air that came from outside to replace it wasn't much cooler.

Rhodes had forgotten to open his cardboard sunscreen and set it in the windshield, and the sun shining through the glass had heated the ignition lock to something just short of the melting point. When Rhodes shoved in the key, it immediately became almost too hot to hold.

As soon as the car started, Rhodes turned the air conditioner down as cold as it would go and turned the fan on high. It took awhile, but eventually the interior of the car became cool enough for Rhodes to breathe without fear of scorching his lungs.

Driving out to the precinct barn, he went through downtown Clearview, only a few blocks from the courthouse. One block of old buildings had recently been cleared away, and now a brand-new chiropractic center and insurance office stood, shining bright and white, where there once had been a café, a drugstore, a dry goods store, a jewelry store, an electrical supply store, and a barbershop.

Several of the old buildings had collapsed because of a combination of old age and general neglect. The others had not been in such bad condition, but they'd been torn down anyway. The old buildings that still stood nearby looked drab and run-down compared with the new ones.

Rhodes supposed it was nice to have some life in the downtown area again, but he hated to see the buildings go. They'd been there all his life, and their decline and fall reminded him uncomfortably of what the passing of time could do to both buildings and people. He told himself that while change was inevitable, that didn't mean he had to like it, especially when it meant getting older and losing his forelock.

He got out of the car at the precinct barn, and the sun shot through his thinning hair like a molten bullet. It was almost enough to make Rhodes wish he wore a hat. But he didn't like hats, and in fact he was probably the only sheriff in Texas who didn't wear a felt Stetson in the fall and winter and a straw hat in the spring and summer. He wondered if there was a rule about not wearing a straw hat after Labor Day.

Rhodes thought he heard sirens in the distance. Probably another grass fire, he thought. He hoped it wasn't a bad one.

He looked out at the precinct barns. Drums of weed-killing poison were stacked along one wall, and pest strips hung from the ceiling. Rhodes thought the strips had been outlawed years earlier, and these were probably leftovers. Bulldozers, tractors, mowers, and road graders sat under a long tin roof, though Rhodes supposed that some of them were out at work. He was glad he wasn't driving one of them. Some of them had little umbrella canopies that provided little or no protection from the sun and none from the heat. Others had nothing at all.

The inside of the precinct office was so cool compared to the outside that it chilled the sweat on Rhodes's skin. He felt for a second as if he'd walked into a meat locker.

Mrs. Wilkie sat behind her desk, tapping away on a computer keyboard. She looked up when Rhodes came in and gave him a professional smile.

"Good morning, Sheriff," she said. "Hot enough for you?"

"Not really," Rhodes said. "I generally like it when it's about ten degrees warmer. Really does my circulation good."

Mrs. Wilkie looked at him as if he might have lost his mind. She said, "I guess you're here to see Mr. Allen."

"That's right. Is he here this morning?"

The door to Allen's office was open, and he had obviously been listening. Without waiting for Mrs. Wilkie to announce Rhodes he came out, shook hands, and told Rhodes to come on in. When they were inside, Allen closed the door.

They sat down and talked for a while about inconsequential things. Rhodes asked about Allen's children, of whom there were, as best Rhodes could recall, seven. Two were in college, and five were still living at home. But one of those was about to go away to college in the fall.

"College is expensive these days," Rhodes said.

"What isn't?" Allen said.

The talk turned to the Fourth of July festivities, and Rhodes admitted that he wouldn't be entering the three-mile fun run again. The fun run had been instituted ten years earlier, and so far Rhodes had an unbroken string of ten years when he hadn't been a part of it. He was shooting for at least twenty-five. He thought that *fun run* was an oxymoron, like *jumbo shrimp* and *Internet privacy*.

"You used to be able to run," Allen said. " 'Will-o'-the wisp Dan Rhodes' is what they called you in the *Herald*, I think."

In his one moment of glory as a high school football player, Rhodes had run a kickoff back for a touchdown, gaining him a nickname that only very few people remembered. Shortly after that run, he'd been injured, and his athletic career had come to an inglorious end.

"That was a long time ago," he said. "I don't think they call anybody will-o'-the-wisp these days."

"No," Allen said. "I'm not sure anyone under the age of forty would know what it meant. They'd probably call you 'Ramblin' Rhodes' now. But I have a feeling you didn't come here to talk over old times at Clearview High."

Rhodes wished he had. He said, "No. It's about something I heard from a reporter."

Allen leaned back in his desk chair and crossed his arms over his chest.

"Jennifer Loam," he said. "I should have known. What did she tell you about me?"

"About you? Nothing. She accused me of using inmates to paint my house."

"What a crock. Roy Dean Turner did that."

"I'm glad you noticed. Can I call you as a witness?"

"You're kidding. She's not going to print some crazy story about you using inmate labor, is she?"

"I hope not. But Ms. Loam is checking out all the angles before she absolves me. You commissioners are another matter."

Allen grinned ruefully. "How well I know."

"So she's talked to you?"

"Among others. I'm not the main suspect."

"Who is?"

"I don't know for sure," Allen said. "But I can tell you who Loam spent the most time with."

"I think I already know," Rhodes said. "She let it slip."

Allen raised his eyebrows and said, "She doesn't strike me as the kind to let anything slip."

"I sort of tricked her. She was upset about the way she was treated by one of the commissioners, and I asked her for a name."

"And she told you."

"Yes. I'm not sure she realized it."

"Not that you'd try to trick me," Allen said, "but why don't you tell me the name."

"You'll tell me if I'm right?"

"Sure. Why not?"

"Jay Beaman," Rhodes said.

Allen nodded. "That would be the one."

"I wonder what she has on him?"

"Maybe nothing at all. She thought she had something on you, remember?"

"She seems to think she has better evidence in Beaman's case. Which reminds me: she said her 'source' was going to provide her with pictures of the inmates painting my house. I wonder if she was promised something like that in Beaman's case."

"You mean she might not have the evidence yet?" Allen said.

"I thought from what she said that she'd seen the evidence on the commissioner," Rhodes said. "But now I think I could have been wrong."

"Let's hope so. We really don't need any scandals around here."

Rhodes had a cynical feeling he knew why Allen felt that way. Commissioners were generally about as secure in their positions as any politician ever got. Some of them spent decades on the job without ever having an opponent. They managed to build up so much money on campaign contributions that a newcomer didn't really have a chance to compete. About the only thing that an incumbent had to fear was some kind of scandal.

Before Rhodes could put his thoughts into words, there was a timid knock on the office door. Allen got up, walked around his desk, and opened the door. Rhodes turned his head to see Mrs. Wilkie standing there.

"I hate to interrupt," she said, "but there's a phone call for the sheriff."

"He can take it in here," Allen said.

Mrs. Wilkie nodded and said, "Line one."

Allen went back to the desk and picked up the telephone. He handed the receiver to Rhodes. There was a clear plastic button on the base, with a blinking red light inside. Allen pressed the button.

"Hello," Rhodes said. "This is the sheriff."

"I know who it is," Hack said. "I'm the one who phoned you."

"What's the trouble?" Rhodes asked.

"Fire," Hack said.

Rhodes remembered the sirens he'd heard earlier.

"I don't usually get called about fires," he said.

"You do when they're bad ones."

"How bad is this one?"

"Somebody's dead," Hack said. "That bad enough for you?"

"It'll do," Rhodes said.

5

Rhodes drove out of town towards Milsby, which by coincidence was the area in which Mrs. Wilkie lived. Milsby had been a town once, but there wasn't much left of it now, just an old school building, the ragged remains of a couple of stores, and some houses. Rhodes hoped Clearview wouldn't look like that in another fifty years. He didn't think it would. Even if everything else passed away, there would always be the Wal-Mart.

Milsby was also the place where Rhodes had more than once encountered a biker named Rapper, a man who'd caused more than his share of trouble in Blacklin County, though he'd never served time in jail for any of it. Rhodes wondered if Rapper was back and if he had anything to do with the fire. It seemed unlikely. While Rapper hadn't done any jail time, he'd suffered quite a bit on each of his forays into Rhodes's territory.

Before he got to Milsby, just after he passed the Clearview city limits sign, Rhodes saw a fireworks stand, one of many safely located in an unincorporated area of the county, where fireworks were legal. The stand was little more than a tin shed, painted yellow — and most of the year it was closed — with two wings that folded in from each side enclosing the interior. The word FIREWORKS was painted on the wings in black, and there was a picture of an exploding firecracker at each end of it.

The wings were opened before Christmas each year, and they were kept open until January first. They were also opened several weeks before the Fourth of July, as they were now, and an array of explosive materials was revealed: cherry bombs, bottle rockets, Roman candles, firecrackers, sparklers, and whistlers, all wrapped in colorful paper and ready for lighting.

Rhodes could remember the times he'd popped firecrackers as a kid, doing dangerous things like putting them under cans or holding them until the fuse nearly burned down and then throwing them. It had seemed like an innocent pastime, but he was lucky he hadn't been injured. He was lucky he hadn't started a fire.

There was a banner hanging over the stand that said BUY 1, GET 5 FREE! It sounded like quite a bargain, and Rhodes wondered how the owner of the stand could make any money. But he was making money, all right. He wouldn't be there in that heat if he weren't.

Two cars were parked in front of the stand. Rhodes supposed he could call a deputy and have the cars followed. If they went back into Clearview, the drivers could be fined, since fireworks were illegal within the city limits. But by the time a deputy arrived, the cars would be gone.

Rhodes couldn't make out the face of the worker under the canopy of the stand, but whoever it was gave the sheriff an ironic salute as he drove by.

Rhodes nodded and kept going. He wondered what the man thought about the fire. Or if he even cared.

The county car's air conditioner wasn't set on *recirculate,* and Rhodes could smell the fire long before he got to it, the acrid odor of smoke from burned grass, trees, and fence posts filling the car.

When Rhodes topped a little hill, he could see that the fire wasn't entirely out. The three Clearview fire trucks were on the scene, and the pumper truck must still have had a little water left in it. Rhodes could see a silver stream spraying out over the line of flames in the grass. There were men slapping at stray flames with wet burlap bags.

The fire had destroyed several acres, now scorched black, and burned an old frame house that stood on one side. A small metal shed had been spared, but nothing much was left of the house. Some charred boards were still upright, and the singed bricks of a chimney were scattered around the yard. The roof had mostly fallen in.

There was something else left, too, according

to what Hack had told Rhodes, but that was inside the house.

Rhodes drove into the gate and stopped the car near one of the fire trucks. He got out. The burned grass crunched under his feet, and ash puffed up around his shoes.

The fire, what was left of it, was a good distance away, but the thought of it made Rhodes feel even hotter. He started sweating immediately.

Gary Parker, the fire chief, saw Rhodes and came over. He was a big man with a brown, seamed face and watery blue eyes. Sweat was running down his face, which was streaked with soot, and Rhodes thought he must be basting in his own juices inside the heavy fire-fighting clothing.

"Wasn't much we could do," Parker told Rhodes. "Deserted area like this, it didn't get called in till the house was about gone. Somebody passing by used a cell phone."

"How'd it start?" Rhodes asked. "Any ideas?"

Parker turned and pointed toward the road.

"Well," he said, "you can see that it burned toward the fence line, even got some of the posts. But it didn't get to the bar ditch. We got here before it could."

He turned back and indicated the line where the men were still fighting the remaining flames.

"And over there it almost got to that little woods. But we've pretty much stopped it."

"What does that tell us?" Rhodes asked.

45

"Have to do a complete investigation, naturally," Parker said. "Even then we might not know for sure. But it looks like it started in the house."

"There's a body in the house?"

"That's right. Burned pretty bad. We left him there for you."

"What about an ambulance?"

"Should be on the way," Parker said, and almost as soon as he spoke, Rhodes heard a siren in the distance.

"There it comes now," Parker said. "It's not for that guy in there, though."

"Who, then?"

"George Dobbs. One of my guys. Heat was too much for him. He passed out. He's lying in the shade of one of the trucks right now."

"He going to be okay?"

"Sure. That kind of thing happens all the time when the weather's like this. I haven't lost anybody yet. Come close a couple of times, though."

The ambulance pulled through the gate, and Rhodes saw someone motioning it over toward one of the fire trucks.

"Do you have any idea who owns this property?" Rhodes asked. He thought he knew the answer, but he wasn't sure. If Parker didn't know, Rhodes could check with Hack.

"Not the faintest," Parker said. "Nice place, though. Good bass-fishing tank back in those trees."

"Any way I can get a look at the body?"

"I guess it's not too dangerous now. You don't have to go inside the house. The whole wall on the side where the bedroom was is gone. You can look at him from there. You'll have to put on some protective gear, though."

"Do you have any to spare?"

"Yeah. I'll show you where. Then I got to see about George. Wouldn't want him to be the first one I lost."

"Me neither," Rhodes said.

The smell of wet, burned wood was strong, but not strong enough. Rhodes could still smell the faint but unmistakable odor of cooked flesh.

He stood in the soaked cinders and hoped he wasn't going to pass out the way George Dobbs had done. It was hotter than hell's back forty in the fire-fighting gear.

He could see well enough, however. Maybe too well. The burned body lay on what had once been a mattress. Under the remains of the mattress, which seemed to Rhodes to be still smoldering, was a mostly melted set of springs. Of the bed itself there was hardly a trace. The fire had been really hot at that point, and Rhodes wondered if it had started there. Smoking in bed, maybe. An old story, but one that was always in fashion.

The body wasn't recognizable. It looked almost like a skeleton with papery black skin

47

stretched over it, and the skin appeared so loosely attached that a good breeze might peel it right off the bones beneath. There were no eyes. The mouth was open, and Rhodes could see teeth. So the body could be identified, eventually. Rhodes had a feeling he'd find out who it was long before any dental records were looked at, however.

He moved a little closer and picked up a blackened stick. He knew that he shouldn't poke around in the ashes too much. There was always the danger of stirring up a spark that would set the whole thing going again. But he saw something that he wanted to have a better look at, and raking it up with a stick would be a good bit safer than tromping around in the ashes in the overlarge pair of boots he'd borrowed. They slipped up and down on his heels, and he felt clumsy walking in them on level ground. So there was no way he was going into the cinders with them on his feet. He might fall, start a new fire, and be a cinder himself before anyone could do anything about it.

Using the stick, Rhodes pulled the object toward him. It appeared to be a bottle of some kind, most likely a whiskey bottle, judging from its shape. It wasn't melted. Maybe it had been under the bed and partially protected from the worst of the fire.

He fished the bottle out of the ashes, poked the stick in the neck, and looked at it. A whiskey bottle for sure, he thought. Drinking and smoking in bed, it seemed like. Not a good combination.

Except why would somebody be drinking and smoking early in the day?

He thought he had an answer to that question. The drinking had been done during the night, and the smoking, too. Whoever had been in the bed could have been passing the time, waiting for daylight to go fishing in the little stock tank in the woods. It could take quite a while for a dropped cigarette to set a mattress afire.

Rhodes had seen enough. He wanted to talk to Hack, and he wanted to get out of the fire-fighting clothes. He figured that he'd probably lost ten pounds by now, but he'd gain it back as soon as he could find about ten Dr Peppers. He left the whiskey bottle where it was. Chief Parker could draw his own conclusions when he did his investigation. And of course the justice of the peace would have to come and pronounce the body dead. Rhodes didn't have any doubts about that himself.

"That's the old Parsons place," Hack said, his voice sounding a bit crackly on the radio. "I remember when Norv Parsons ran cattle on those acres. That was a long time ago, though."

Rhodes realized that time didn't matter as far as the name of the place was concerned. It could change hands fifty times and people of Hack's generation would still call it "the old Parsons place."

"Who owns it now?" Rhodes asked.

"I think Grat Bilson bought it last year."

"I was afraid you were going to tell me that," Rhodes said.

6

Rhodes had thought he remembered something about Grat Bilson's buying the old Parsons place, and with Hack's confirmation, he knew he'd remembered correctly. The talk around town was that Bilson had bought the land because he wanted a place to go fishing and, so people said, get away from his wife.

Bilson was well known around Clearview. He owned a small electrical repair shop and worked as much or as little as he pleased. He spent his spare time fighting with his wife, fishing, and working with the Sons and Daughters of Texas, not necessarily in that order. In his younger days, he'd played football for the Clearview High Catamounts, and his interest in county history had kept his name in the papers in recent years. He was also concerned about the environment, which had led to his current preoccupation with getting some kind of fireworks ban enacted for the county.

Rhodes had a feeling that Bilson would be getting his name in the papers one more time, but that he wouldn't be around to enjoy the publicity. It seemed likely that it was his body in the bed.

He was about to drive back to Clearview when another car pulled through the gate. It drove right up beside Rhodes and stopped. Jennifer Loam got out.

"I was covering some stupid 'color the flag' contest at Wal-Mart," she said. "No one thought to call me about this until now. What happened?"

"There was a fire," Rhodes said. "It's about all over."

That was true. The firemen were gathered around the trucks, still looking watchful, though it appeared that all the flames had been extinguished.

"I can see there was a fire," Jennifer said. "But there's something about a body."

"Someone was in the house."

"Who?"

"I don't know. The only way we'll get a positive identification is through dental records."

"It was Grat Bilson, wasn't it."

Rhodes wondered how she'd arrived at the conclusion.

"There's no way to tell for sure," he said.

"This was his place," Jennifer said. "He came out here to fish and get a little peace and quiet."

For someone who was fairly new in town, she seemed to know a lot about Grat Bilson. He was a prominent citizen, and he was active in civic affairs, but not everyone would know about his private life. But someone who'd been talking to him in secret would.

"I didn't know you were acquainted with Grat," Rhodes said.

"I . . . he was president of one of those historical societies. I interviewed him once."

Rhodes couldn't remember reading any interview with Bilson in the paper.

"He was your source, wasn't he," Rhodes said.

Jennifer shook her head but then seemed to change her mind. She said, "Okay, you're right. How did you know?"

"I figured it out, and you're not very convincing when you're not telling the truth. You must have come out here to meet with him. That's how you knew why he bought it."

Jennifer was silent for a while, as if thinking over how much she wanted to tell Rhodes. Finally she said, "You're right. Hardly anyone ever drives by here, and it seemed like a good place to meet. He didn't want us to be seen together, and of course I didn't want to compromise my source."

"If he's dead, he won't be a source anymore. That could be a problem for your story."

"I don't see how."

"Did you have corroboration for everything he told you?" Rhodes asked.

Jennifer shook her head and said, "You sound like one of my old journalism professors."

Rhodes had never thought of himself as being very professorial. He didn't feel that way now, either. And he didn't like the sound of the word *old*.

"I don't know much about journalism," he said, "but I do know that you can't print anything without corroboration."

"People do it," Jennifer said, a little defensively.

"And they usually get caught. What happens then isn't very pretty. You wouldn't want it to happen to you. So the question is, do you have it?"

"I have it," Jennifer said. "Well, sort of."

" 'Sort of' doesn't count. It doesn't even come close."

"I know that. I didn't mean it the way it sounded. I have plenty."

"For example?"

"I think I told you before: you'll have to read about it in the *Herald*."

"So you're going ahead with the story?"

"Sure," Jennifer said. "I'm sorry Mr. Bilson's dead, if he's the one who died. But that doesn't change anything about the story. On the record, do you know what started the fire?"

Rhodes was a little taken aback by the sudden change in subject until he noticed that a tiny tape recorder had suddenly appeared in Jennifer's hand. He said, "I don't know, and neither does Chief Parker. There'll be an investigation, as usual in these cases."

"Is there suspicion of foul play?"

Rhodes thought about it. He hadn't been suspicious at first, but that was before he learned that Bilson had been telling Jennifer things about the commissioners. Was it possible that someone had killed him to shut him up? Rhodes didn't think so. Surely the commissioners of such a small county didn't have that much to hide.

"No," he said. "Right now it looks like an accidental death. There'll be an autopsy, though, and we'll see what that tells us."

"Do you think there's any connection between this death and the deaths of Faye Knape and Ty Berry?"

Berry and Knape had been the presidents of the two historical societies before Bilson and Lindsay, and they'd both been killed a while back, before Jennifer had moved to Clearview. But she was a woman who did her research, and it wasn't surprising that she knew about the deaths of the society presidents. Rhodes figured it was going to be hard to get anyone to take Bilson's job, what with Bilson's being the third president to die within the last couple of years. Not that being president of any organization had a thing to do with the deaths, but who'd want to take the chance?

"No connection at all," Rhodes said. "Let's try not to scare anyone by bringing that up. We know who killed Knape and Berry, and, as I said, this looks like an accident."

"But there'll be a thorough investigation?"

Rhodes smiled at that. He never turned down the chance to let the voters know what a great job he was doing.

"There always is," he said.

7

Rhodes finished the impromptu interview and left Jennifer to tackle Chief Parker. He drove back to town, passing by the fireworks stand on the way. There were four cars parked in front this time, and Rhodes got another salute from the person behind the counter.

By the time he got to Clearview, it was nearly two o'clock, and Rhodes thought about lunch. He missed lunch a lot, but he usually made up for it in one way or another. He was trying to eat healthier foods these days, and Ivy was a big help in that endeavor. Sometimes Rhodes thought she was too big a help, what with all the tofu-based foods that he found in the refrigerator. Still, he'd lost a little weight, so he couldn't complain. Not that he was fat. It was just that for a while there, it had been a little tricky for him to get a glimpse of his belt buckle. But he could see it just fine now, thank you very much.

At the moment, he wasn't in the mood for tofu, so he wheeled through the drive-through window at McDonald's and got a Big Mac and an order of fries. He got water to drink, not because he was cutting down on calories but because he didn't like ice-diluted soft drinks.

He drove to the city park, where the Fourth of July celebrations would take place in a couple of days, and parked under a shade tree to eat his burger. There was no one in the park because it was far too hot to be swinging or seesawing or riding the merry-go-round.

Sitting there under the tree with the car windows rolled down, Rhodes tried to pretend that there was enough of a breeze to keep him cool.

He remembered the days when he'd played in that same park. The old concrete-and-stone bandstand was still there, but it was too small for a band. There had been a shuffleboard game painted on the floor when Rhodes was young, but he doubted that it still existed. The paint would have worn off long ago, and what kid would want to play shuffleboard now? It couldn't compare with Sony's video games.

The softball field was there, too, with the dead outfield grass almost worn down to the bare ground. Rhodes had shagged a lot of flies there in the days when he was collecting baseball cards and trying to get a complete set of the year's offering from Topps. He wondered how long it had been since he'd swung a bat or put on a baseball glove. Too long to remember, but the smell of the leather and the sound of a wooden bat hitting the ball were as clear as if it had been yesterday.

Rhodes finished his meal and went by the jail to see if anything needed his attention. Hack said nothing much was going on, but he wanted to know about the fire.

"You think that's Grat Bilson's body they found?" he asked.

"Could be," Rhodes said. "But I don't know that. We'll have to check the dental records to be sure."

"What about the cause of death?"

"We'll have to wait for an autopsy. It looked like a case of smoking in bed."

Rhodes's conversation with Jennifer Loam had made him wonder if there might be more to it than that, but there was no need to go into that idea with Hack, at least not at the moment.

"Too bad," Hack said. "Grat was a pretty good fella, most of the time. Him and his wife sure didn't get along, though. You goin' to talk to her?"

Rhodes said that he was.

"Gonna ask her if Grat was out at that old house last night?"

"That's why I'm going to talk to her."

"I wonder how she'll take the news?"

"It might not have been Grat, so there might not be any news."

"Yeah, yeah. But what if it *was* him? How do you think she'll take it?"

Rhodes didn't know the answer to that. Everyone knew that Yvonne Bilson wasn't exactly a stay-at-home wife who devoted herself to cooking, cleaning, and creating arts and crafts. One of the things she and Grat fought about was her numerous flings with other men. Somehow, their marriage had survived her wanderings, but it hadn't been easy on either of them.

"She prob'ly won't be too upset if it's Grat," Hack said. "She might even thank you for bringin' the news. Wonder if Grat had a will."

"I guess we'll find out," Rhodes said. "Are you implying that there might be something suspicious about the death?"

Hack raised his hands and shook his head.

"Not me. I'm not implyin' anything. I'm not the sheriff. It's not my job to investigate stuff and come to conclusions about it. They don't pay me enough for that. I just answer the phone."

Hack had the perfect confidence man's deadpan face and voice, but Rhodes had been working with him too long to buy the act. The dispatcher obviously knew something, but he'd never come right out and say it. No, that wasn't the way it worked. Hack would prefer to have Rhodes beg him for information, but Rhodes wouldn't go that far. So Hack would string him along as far as he could before actually parting with any details of what he knew. Rhodes was willing to play along for a while, at least until he lost his patience.

"Is there anything you've heard about Grat and Yvonne Bilson lately?" Rhodes asked. "Anything about them you'd like to tell me?"

While Rhodes was asking his question, Lawton came in from the cell block and quietly closed the door behind him. He crossed his

59

arms, leaned back against the wall, and stood there listening.

"Well," Hack said, "you know how it is. A man hears things, but that don't mean they're true. Could be just rumors. I don't like to repeat rumors."

"I know how it pains you," Rhodes said. "But just this once wouldn't hurt."

"What rumor is it that you want to hear?" Lawton asked. "I don't mind repeatin' a good story, myself, and I hear as much as Hack does."

Hack turned and glared at him. "Nobody asked you to butt in. This is my story, and I'll be the one to tell it."

"Wouldn't want you to go against your ethical principles," Lawton said. "Wouldn't want you to compromise your integrity when it comes to passin' along unsubstantiated gossip."

"You don't even know what those words mean," Hack said. "You couldn't spell *unsubstantiated* if your life was to depend on it."

"Maybe not. I don't have me one of those fancy computers that tells me when I spell something wrong like the one the county bought for you. But I have ears, and I do hear some of the gossip that goes on around town. I don't have to be able to spell Yvonne Bilson's name to know that she's been runnin' around with —"

"Jay Beaman," Hack said before Lawton could beat him to it.

Maybe Rhodes should have been surprised, but he wasn't. In fact, it made sense. Grat Bilson had always seemed to hate his wife's tendency to make friends so easily, but he'd never done anything much about it, other than argue with her. Sometimes the arguments got loud, with lots of name-calling, but they never got violent, and for whatever reason, neither Grat nor Yvonne had ever considered divorce, at least not as far as Rhodes knew.

But if Yvonne had been playing around with Jay Beaman, Grat might have changed his methods. He might very well have turned to Jennifer Loam in an attempt to get back at both Yvonne and Jay. The president of the United States might be able to get away with a certain amount of slap and tickle, or even quite a bit of it, and the electorate would overlook his behavior even if the Congress didn't. A county commissioner, however, couldn't count on that kind of forgiveness from the voters, and come the next election, he might find himself losing a job he thought would be his until he retired or died, whichever came first. It wouldn't be hard for Bilson to provide the corroboration Rhodes had mentioned to Jennifer Loam, either.

On the other hand, the editor of the Clearview *Herald* wasn't likely to print a story alleging adultery by one of the commissioners if that was the only thing that Beaman was involved in. There had to be more to it than that.

"Yvonne Bilson has messed around with half

the men in the county," Rhodes said. "That's not exactly big news."

"Hasn't ever messed around with me," Lawton said.

"Don't blame her," Hack said. "Who'd want to mess around with the likes of you?"

"Maybe Miz McGee would," Lawton said, referring to the woman with whom Hack was keeping company. "She's prob'ly tired of an old sourpuss like you by now."

Hack's face went red, and Rhodes knew it was time to step in before Hack popped a blood vessel and died right there in the office. Teasing Hack was fine, as long as you didn't cross the line and bring Miz McGee into it.

"All right," Rhodes said, "let's break it up."

"He oughtn't talk about Miz McGee like that," Hack said.

"He knows that. Right, Lawton?"

Lawton did his best to look contrite, but Rhodes suspected that he wasn't chastened in the least.

"Yeah," Lawton said. "I know better'n that. Miz McGee's a fine woman. It's just that she's too good for the fella that she's going with."

Hack stood up. There was a little vein standing out on his forehead, and Rhodes was afraid that he might be on the verge of a stroke.

"You've got Hack so upset that it makes me wonder," Rhodes said.

"Wonder what?" Lawton asked.

"How worked up a man can get about a

woman," Rhodes said. "And whether a man would kill for Yvonne Bilson."

Hack took a deep breath, and his face got a shade paler. The little vein stopped throbbing.

"Are you sayin' that Commissioner Beaman might've burned Grat Bilson up?" he asked.

"What?" Lawton said, his eyes wide. "Is Grat dead? Is there something goin' on here I don't know about?"

Hack realized then that he was one up on Lawton, and the look of anger on his face was replaced by something resembling satisfaction.

"Me and the sheriff were just talkin' about that," Hack said. "I guess you don't know as much as you think you do about what's goin' on around here."

"Well, I sure do wish somebody would fill me in, then. It's not right to keep me in the dark when ever'body else knows what's happenin'."

"You may not have a high enough security clearance for this information," Hack said. "What about it, Sheriff?"

"I guess he could be told," Rhodes said. "But you'll have to do it. I'm going to see Yvonne."

"You better watch out for her," Hack said. "She might want to mess around with you."

"I don't mess around, boy," Rhodes said, in his best Ricky Nelson voice, which even he had to admit was none too good.

8

The Bilsons lived in one of Clearview's "new" additions, which meant that their house was only about ten years old. Building wasn't exactly on the boom in Blacklin County.

Rhodes parked in front of the brick home with its mailbox on a pole in front. Someone had been watering the grass, which wasn't as dead as that in Rhodes's yard. There was still a good bit of green in it, so it had probably been fertilized as well, and it was neatly mown and edged. There were flower beds in front of the house with carefully tended rosebushes. Rhodes didn't know the names of the roses. They were red and yellow, which was enough for him.

Rhodes went to the door and pushed the bell button. The chimes played the first few notes of "I've Been Workin' on the Railroad." Either that, or "The Eyes of Texas." It all depended on your point of view, Rhodes supposed.

Yvonne Bilson opened the door. She was thin, almost too thin, and nearly as tall as Rhodes, one of the few women he knew who didn't have to tilt her head to look him in the face. Her white shirt and jeans fit her like the clothes of a scarecrow. She had a cigarette between the first two fingers of her right hand, and while she looked Rhodes over, she took a puff and blew a plume of white smoke in his direction.

"What's the son of a bitch done this time?" she asked.

Rhodes recalled that *son of a bitch* was one of Yvonne's favorite phrases, one that she didn't use exclusively when referring to Grat. She'd called Rhodes that on more than one occasion, but he was pretty sure that this time she meant Grat.

"Can I come in?" he said.

"Sure, why not," Yvonne said. "Nobody here but me and Alex Trebek."

She let Rhodes into a small living room that was dominated by a thirty-two-inch TV set on which three *Jeopardy* contestants were confronted with the answer, "He wrote *The Autobiography of Malcolm X* before he discovered his roots."

"Alex Haley," Yvonne said before a contestant buzzed in.

"Not bad," Rhodes said when she proved to be right.

"Men like women with brains," Yvonne said.

Rhodes wondered if that was her secret, since her physical appearance didn't seem to provide a clue. But then he wasn't much of a judge.

"You can have a seat if you want to," Yvonne said, turning off the TV set with the remote.

Maybe it wasn't her brain, Rhodes thought. Maybe it was her gracious manners.

He looked around the room for a place to sit. There was a couch, a recliner, and a wooden straight-backed rocker to choose from. He sat in the rocker, and Yvonne sat on the couch where she could reach the nearly full ashtray on the coffee table. The whole house smelled like smoke.

"You still haven't told me what the son of a bitch did," Yvonne said.

"If you're talking about Grat, I'm not sure whether he did anything. Did he go out to his fishing place last night?"

Yvonne stubbed out her cigarette and picked up a package of Marlboros and a red plastic lighter from the coffee table. She shook a cigarette out of the pack and lit it.

"Yeah, he went out there," she said, exhaling smoke. "Said he needed to think about his part in the Fourth of July jamboree. I don't know what there was to think about. All he does is the announcing. He just reads what they give him, and they haven't given him anything yet. You'd think he could stay here and read over it anyway."

Rhodes wondered why Grat had left, too. It seemed to Rhodes that if a man's wife were straying, the man might want to stay at home with her. Maybe she wouldn't go anywhere if he was there. Or maybe that was too simple an answer to be worth anything.

"Have you heard from him today?"

"Who, Grat? Why should I hear from him? What's the matter? What's he done?"

"Does Grat drink much?"

"Drink? Of course he drinks. You can't live without drinking. The body's more than ninety percent water, you know."

Rhodes said he didn't know but that he wasn't talking about water.

"You mean liquor, then? I guess he drank a little. Everybody drinks a little. Well, maybe sheriffs don't. But everybody else does. Why? Why are you asking all these questions?"

Rhodes hated to tell her what he had to say next. In all his years in law enforcement, he had never found a good way to tell someone that a relative or friend was dead, and in this case it might not even be true. He hated to alarm someone unnecessarily. But he didn't see anything else to do, so he went ahead.

"There was a fire out there at the house near Grat's fishing hole," he said. "The whole house burned."

"Grat," Yvonne said. "What about Grat?"

"The firemen found a body in the house. I don't know that it's Grat. That's what I'm trying to find out."

"That son of a bitch!" Yvonne said. She threw her cigarette in the ashtray. "That son of a bitch! He can't do this to me. He can't go and die on me! It's not right!"

And then she started to cry. Not quietly, not with gentle sobs, but with great gasps and wailing. Rhodes had never seen anyone react quite so frenziedly to the news that her husband might be dead.

In fact, Yvonne was so wracked with sobbing that Rhodes didn't know quite what to do, and he found himself going to the couch, sitting beside her, and putting his arms around her, which was really out of the ordinary for him and made him feel vaguely uncomfortable.

His comforting, such as it was, didn't help. Yvonne continued to cry, and her body jerked spasmodically. Rhodes was afraid she might have some kind of seizure, but he kept on sitting there, holding her and hoping that she would eventually cry herself out.

It happened, but it took awhile. Rhodes was in no position to check his watch, but he was sure the crying went on for at least five minutes. Finally it subsided, and the jerking slowed down to nothing more than hiccups.

Rhodes released Yvonne and said, "I'll get you a drink of water."

He didn't ask where the kitchen was. He figured he could find it, and he didn't want Yvonne to try to tell him. He was sure that she couldn't complete a sentence.

The kitchen was, in fact, easy enough to find. Rhodes opened a cabinet, found a glass, and filled it at the tap. He found a roll of paper towels and tore off a couple. Then he took the water and the towels back into the living room and handed the towels to Yvonne. She used them to dry her face, and a lot of her makeup came off on them. She crumpled them into a ball and threw them on the coffee table.

Rhodes gave her the water. Her hand still was shaky, and she slopped a little of the water into the ashtray, but Rhodes thought that was a good thing. The water put out the still-smoldering cigarette that she had dropped there. It wouldn't do to have another Bilson burning down a house and dying in the fire, especially not right after a visit with the sheriff. Much less while he was still there.

Yvonne drank the entire glass of water and set the empty glass on the coffee table. Rhodes thought that it would probably make a ring, but that didn't seem worth mentioning at the moment.

"Are you going to be all right?" he asked.

Yvonne hiccupped and said, "Yes."

Rhodes wasn't sure he should believe her. Her eyes were red, and her face was haggard.

"Is there someone I can call?" he asked.

"No. I'll call somebody myself. When you're gone."

Rhodes could recognize subtle hints when he heard them, but he was good at ignoring them. He said, "I know it's upsetting to think that Grat might be dead. But he might not be. The body hasn't been identified."

"It's him. It's just like the son of a bitch to go kill himself and leave me alone."

Judging from all he'd heard about Yvonne, Rhodes didn't think she'd be alone for very long. However, after the display she'd just put on, he wasn't sure.

On the other hand, he wondered if the weeping had all been nothing but a big show for his benefit. Maybe he was getting too cynical, but Yvonne had never demonstrated much affection for Grat in the past, and she was one person who'd known for sure where he was the previous night. What if she'd decided to get rid of him once and for all, with the idea that no one would ever suspect a woman who was so overwhelmed with grief and who seemed to believe that her husband had killed himself?

Rhodes decided that he shouldn't be thinking along those lines. While he was pretty sure that Grat's body was the one that had been found, there was no reason to suspect that he'd been murdered. Yet.

"I don't think whoever it was killed himself. It might not have been Grat. We don't know for sure."

"How did he die, then? Whoever he was."

"It looks like an accident, like he was smoking in bed and drinking heavily. He must've dropped a cigarette onto the mattress."

"That sounds like a good possibility. There's just one thing wrong with it, as far as Grat's concerned."

"What?" Rhodes asked.

"Grat didn't smoke," Yvonne said.

9

Rhodes wasn't sure what to make of his visit with Yvonne Bilson. The more he thought about her behavior, the more he wondered how much of it had been real and how much had been for show.

The way she had questioned him when he first mentioned Grat's name, for example, was a little bothersome. What was that all about? Was she simply concerned about her husband, or was she setting Rhodes up for all the moaning and wailing that were to come later?

One thing was certain, however. The fact that Grat didn't smoke made it a lot more likely that the fire hadn't been accidental.

It was easier than people thought to set up something that looked like an accidental death, as Rhodes knew from some of his recent experiences. It was one thing to set something up, however; fooling everyone involved was a different matter.

Yvonne had been feeling somewhat better when Rhodes left. She was, or claimed to be, convinced that the dead man couldn't be Grat. After all, if he didn't smoke, he couldn't very well have burned himself up by smoking in bed.

She didn't mention the other possibility, the one that was worrying Rhodes; that the body was Grat's, all right, but that he'd been murdered. Rhodes didn't bring it up, either. He didn't want to set off another round of grieving, whether real or faked. And he wondered if Yvonne's failure to mention murder was deliberate. Had she thought that if she didn't bring it up, Rhodes wouldn't think of it on his own?

There were some other nettlesome questions. If the body wasn't Grat, who was it? And where was Grat? If it was Grat, or even if it wasn't, what had caused the fire?

Rhodes didn't like questions like those.

Ballinger's Funeral Home was located in a well-preserved example of what once would have been called a mansion. The grounds had held both a swimming pool and tennis courts, luxuries found at no other home in Clearview. For that matter, no other home in Clearview even had grounds.

Clyde Ballinger had bought the place after the death of the last member of the family who had owned it, and converted the mansion into his funeral home.

It had been a good choice. There was nothing somber about the place. The tennis courts and swimming pool were long gone, but the oak trees in front of the building remained, and the tall white columns on the porch recalled an earlier, simpler time.

Rhodes drove around to the back, where Ballinger had his office in a brick building that had once served as the servants' quarters, in the days when there had been one or two people in Clearview rich enough to have servants.

The door was closed, and there was no bell, so Rhodes knocked. Ballinger was inside and called for him to come in. The office was not where Ballinger met his potential clients. That was inside the main building. This place was his personal refuge, and it was where he went when he wanted to get away from his business and relax for a minute or two. It was littered with paperback books, most of them forty years old or older and most of them by writers Rhodes had never heard of. Ballinger picked the books up at garage sales and flea markets and claimed he liked to read them because they were short.

"Not a hundred and fifty pages of story and five hundred pages of padding like the books they write these days," he'd once told Rhodes. "You get the hundred and fifty pages of story, and that's it."

Rhodes didn't have a lot of time for reading, so he'd never found out for himself. He just took Ballinger's word for it.

When Rhodes walked through the door, Ballinger said, "Hot enough for you?"

"I've already been told I can't go around shooting people for saying that," Rhodes told him. "Otherwise, you'd be one of your own customers."

73

"I'm training somebody to take care of me," Ballinger said. "I want to look natural."

He picked up a book from his desk and held it so that Rhodes could see the cover. It looked more like a magazine than a book, and it was called *Body and Passion*. Below the title, a red-haired woman in a low-cut yellow dress reclined on a couch or bed of some kind. Her fear-filled face stared off the cover at the reader. She wasn't wearing any shoes. Beside the bed was an apprehensive-looking man, shirt collar undone and bow tie drooping down. He was also staring at something. Behind them was a circular mirror, and reflected in it was what appeared to be a dapper mummy in a tuxedo. Rhodes figured that the man and woman were supposed to be looking at the mummy, who must have walked in on them.

"They don't write 'em like this anymore," Ballinger said. "But they ought to."

"Why's that?" Rhodes asked.

"Because they're like real life," Ballinger said. "Sort of. See, the guy all wrapped up in bandages has been in this big fire. He survived, but he's burned so bad that nobody knows who he is. And to top it all off, he's got amnesia. Even *he* doesn't know who he is."

"So you're telling me that the man from Grat Bilson's place is alive?" Rhodes said. "All wrapped up in bandages at the hospital?"

Ballinger put the book down on his desk beside a stack of others.

"Nope, I'm not telling you that. Whoever they brought in here about a half hour ago is dead as he can get. But the point is, we don't know who it is, do we?"

"No, we don't," Rhodes said.

"Wonder if it'll turn out the way it did in the book."

"The man in the book was alive."

"Yeah. But in the book there were two men in the place that burned down. One of them was dead, and one was alive. Nobody knew which was which."

"You didn't mention that part."

"Well, now I am."

"Are you trying to tell me that there were two people in the fire at Grat's place?"

"No, but it would sure be interesting if there were, wouldn't it?"

"I don't need that kind of interest," Rhodes said. "I think the one body is going to be trouble enough."

"I called Hack. He said you were out talking to Mrs. Bilson."

"I talked to her. She's convinced that it's not Grat's body."

"I'd just about bet that it is. Who else could it be? He owned that place out there and spent a good bit of time there. Has anyone else turned up missing today?"

"Not that I've heard about."

"There you are, then."

"I think we'd better wait for a positive ID before we make up our minds about who's dead and who's not. Have you called Dr. White?"

"He'll do the autopsy tonight. I called Dr. Lewis, too."

Dr. Lewis was one of Clearview's two dentists. There had been another one, a Dr. Samuel Martin, but he'd been killed a few years earlier, after having a curse put on him by someone who rented a house from him.

"Thanks," Rhodes said. "Sometimes I think the county pays me too much, what with you doing most of the hard work."

Ballinger gave a dismissive wave.

"Think nothing of it. Glad to do it. I knew you'd need the dental records and someone to do the examination. Lewis was Bilson's dentist, so he was the logical guy."

Rhodes didn't ask how Ballinger knew who Bilson's dentist was. He said, "I wonder if this will have any effect on the Fourth of July activities."

"If it's Bilson, it will. The historical societies will be in a real tizzy, and they run the show."

"There weren't going to be any fireworks, anyway."

"Yeah, but there was going to be a fun run, and the historical pageant. Not to mention the crafts show and the band concert."

"The show must go on."

"We'll see," Ballinger said.

Back at the jail, Rhodes let Hack fill him in on what else was happening in the county.

"Got a call from down around Thurston," Hack said. "Lots of shootin' goin' on."

Hack, and Lawton when he was there, delighted in being as vague as possible in order to keep Rhodes guessing for as long as they could. Rhodes sometimes suspected that they had a secret plot to drive him crazy, but he hadn't been able to prove it.

"Shooting in town or outside of town?" he asked.

"Pretty close to town. It was Hod Barrett that called it in."

Hod Barrett had a little grocery store in the town of Thurston. He wasn't one of Rhodes's biggest fans.

"Did somebody shoot at Hod?" Rhodes asked.

"Nope. It ain't like we live in Houston, where they have those drive-by shootings. This wasn't like that."

"What was it like?" Rhodes asked.

He knew he wasn't going to get a straight answer, but he thought it was worth a try.

"It was like guns goin' off, *pop, pop, pop,*" Hack said. "Like that."

"I know what guns sound like," Rhodes said, not adding that they didn't go *pop, pop, pop.*

"There were a lot of 'em," Hack said.

"What was going on? A war?"

"You don't have to be sarcastic," Hack said.

"Sorry. I was just wondering if you were going to get to the point."

"You're gettin' mighty touchy these days," Hack said. "Are you feelin' okay?"

"I'm fine," Rhodes said.

"You might try takin' a good multivitamin. I don't think you eat right."

"I think we're getting off the subject," Rhodes said, though he knew that had probably been Hack's intention.

"Maybe so. What were we talkin' about?"

"Guns," Rhodes said. *"Pop, pop, pop."*

"Right. There was a lot of 'em."

"You said that."

"I did? Must be gettin' absentminded in my old age. Anyway, it's the truth."

"What were they shooting at, and who was doing the shooting?"

"Kids," Hack said.

That was a little more specific. Rhodes figured Hack was tired of the game, so he pressed his advantage.

"Kids. Okay. Now, what were they shooting at?"

"Armadillos," Hack said. "There was six or seven kids, prob'ly all about thirteen, all out with their .22s. They must've decided there were too many armadillos around Thurston, and they were goin' to thin the population."

"They should know better than that," Rhodes said. "I hope you got somebody down there before one of them got hurt."

"Ruth's in the area. I gave her a call on the radio. She'll straighten 'em out."

Ruth Grady was one of the deputies, and

Rhodes was sure she'd give the kids a lecture they'd never forget. Most people in Blacklin County were conscious of gun safety, but sometimes adults got careless and kids took advantage. Ruth wouldn't let them off the hook.

"Get Ruth on the radio again," Rhodes said. "Tell her to take up the guns and send the kids home. We'll keep the guns here and make the parents come get them. They can have a lecture, too."

"Ever'body in the county has a .22 in the house," Hack said. "You'll be wastin' your breath."

"It won't be the first time," Rhodes said.

Later that evening, Rhodes was just about to get to bed at a reasonable hour when the telephone rang.

"Let it go," Ivy said.

She was already in the bed, propped up on a pillow and watching the ten o'clock news.

"I'm the sheriff," Rhodes said. "Neither rain nor cold nor dark of night can keep me from my appointed rounds."

"That's the post office," Ivy said as Rhodes picked up the phone, "and besides, you didn't get it quite right."

Rhodes didn't ask for the correct version. He answered the phone, and Dr. White told him he was sorry for calling so late but that he thought Rhodes would like to know what he'd found out about the body from the fire.

"I guess it wasn't anything good," Rhodes said. "Otherwise, you wouldn't be calling."

"That's right. Do you want the long version or the short one?"

"The short one will do."

"There was no smoke in the dead man's lungs," Dr. White said. "You know what that means."

"He was dead before the fire started," Rhodes said.

"That's right."

"But that doesn't mean he didn't die a natural death. He might have had a heart attack."

"He didn't have a heart attack."

Rhodes sighed. "Go ahead and give me the bad news."

"Somebody bashed the back of his head in," Dr. White said. "That's what killed him."

"You're sure?"

"I'm the doctor. I'm sure."

"I'm sorry to hear that," Rhodes said.

He wished he'd been a little more careful with that whiskey bottle.

In fact, he wished he'd been a *lot* more careful.

10

Rhodes was up early the next morning. It was going to be another hot day. The leaves on the pecan trees were drying and curling up in defeat. Pretty soon they'd start dropping off, though it wasn't anywhere near fall.

After letting Yancey chase Speedo around the yard for a while, Rhodes fed and watered both dogs. Then he drove to the Clearview Fire Station.

He had decided that the blow on the head was decisive, and that in the absence of any evidence to the contrary, he was going to assume that Grat Bilson had been murdered and the fire started in an attempt to cover up the killing. The first person he had to talk to was the fire chief.

The fire station wasn't nearly as old as the jail, but it had been built on the cheap in the 1950s, and it wasn't anything to brag about. It was more or less a three-truck garage built of red brick. It had a concrete floor and a small office and living quarters in the rear. The living quarters had concrete floors, too.

Trace Newman, one of the firemen, was washing a truck that he'd driven out of the garage and parked in front.

"Watch your step," he told Rhodes. "Don't slip in the soapy water."

Rhodes said he'd be careful and asked Trace if Parker was there.

"In the office," Trace said. "He thought you might come by."

Rhodes had told Dr. White to call Parker the previous night. He wanted Parker to know what they were getting into. Apparently White had made the call.

The door to the fire chief's office was open, but Rhodes didn't go inside. It was so small that there was hardly room for Parker, his small desk, and his computer. So Rhodes just stood in the doorway until Parker glanced up and saw him.

Parker stood up and said, "Let's go outside and sit on the bench."

It was a tradition in Clearview for benches to be in front of the fire station. When Rhodes had been young, old men had sat there and gossiped in the shade of the lone pecan tree that grew beside the station. Sometimes they would play dominoes on a battered card table. Now, Rhodes supposed, old men had other things to do and other places to go. Maybe they were surfing the Internet or watching cable TV. Rhodes couldn't remember having seen anyone other than a fireman on the bench in many years. In fact, even the firemen didn't sit there now, at least not very often.

Parker sat down in the shade, and Rhodes joined him.

"Wouldn't be so bad if there was a breeze," Parker said.

"Later on, even a breeze won't help," Rhodes said, glad that Parker hadn't asked if it was hot enough for him.

"Probably not," Parker said. "You're here about that dead man, I guess."

"That's right. Dr. White called you?"

"He called. Said it looked like a murder. Good thing I'm a careful man."

Rhodes wasn't sure whether Parker was scolding him or not, but he said, "I got careless myself. I should have hung around and done a thorough crime-scene investigation."

"You did right. The crime was most likely arson-related, so the investigation was my job, and I was glad to do it."

"Did you find anything?"

"If you're asking about clues, I have a whiskey bottle for you, but I don't think it'll be much help."

"You never know," Rhodes said. "I'm glad you saved it."

"Tagged and bagged, as you big-time lawmen say. It's in the office."

"Did you find anything else?"

"Not a thing. That was a pretty hot fire."

"What about that little shed?"

"Well, there was some stuff in there, all right, and there was some stuff missing."

"Missing?" Rhodes said. "How do you know?"

"Well, the only thing in that shed was a few

83

tools and a power mower. That's it. What would you say was missing?"

Rhodes thought it over and said, "What about some gas for the mower?"

"You're a regular Sherlock Holmes. No wonder you're the sheriff. There wasn't any gas, not even an empty gas can."

Which could mean a lot of things, Rhodes realized. But one thing it could mean was that someone took the gas and poured it on Grat, then started the fire.

"That fire was mighty hot where Grat was," Parker said. "That's where it started, right there on that bed. I'm pretty sure that a petroleum accelerant was used, and I'm betting gasoline. But whoever did it might have used the whiskey and then thought of the gasoline later. Those two things together will make a big, hot fire, for sure. We'll know after the testing's done, but right now I can tell you that I'm ruling it a case of arson. Be a nice thing if you could find that gas can, assuming there was one."

Rhodes was sure there had been one. Where it was now, however, was anyone's guess. If the killer had taken it, which seemed likely, it could be at the bottom of a lake or just stuck in a garage where no one would ever notice it. He doubted that there was anything to distinguish it from hundreds of other gas cans all over the county, all of them bought at Wal-Mart, all of them looking exactly alike.

"I don't think the can would help. What we

need is an eyewitness who saw somebody start that fire."

"Won't find anybody like that," Parker said. "Not many folks drive out that way, and that fire was probably started so early that there's no chance at all of anyone having been out that way."

"I'll see what I can turn up," Rhodes said.

"What about his wife?" Parker said. "You think Yvonne did him in?"

"I don't know that it was Grat out there."

"Want to bet it wasn't?"

"No."

Parker grinned. "So, do you think Yvonne did him in?"

"You know what they say on TV."

"I'm not sure. What do they say on TV?"

"Everybody's a suspect," Rhodes told him.

Rhodes's next stop was the offices of the Clearview *Herald*. Jennifer Loam most likely didn't have a source to protect anymore, and Rhodes was going to try charming some information from her.

The *Herald* offices were where they had been for as long as Rhodes could remember, just on the edge of downtown, or what was left of it. Rhodes had delivered the *Herald*, riding all over town on a bicycle and throwing the papers from a canvas bag that he slung across his shoulders. He had been proud of his ability to fold the papers into a flat triangle that he could throw with considerable accuracy. He figured that he hit the porch or front steps more often than not.

On the outside, the *Herald* building didn't look much different from the way it had when Rhodes had gathered at the back door after school with the other paperboys. But the inside of the building was a lot different. Rhodes remembered the Linotype machines and the presses. He remembered the smell of the ink, and he remembered the clattering of machinery, the hum of voices, the clacking of typewriters and a teletype machine.

There was none of that now. The building was almost as quiet as a hospital, and the paper employed only a few people. Computers had changed everything.

Jennifer Loam was at one of the four desks, seated in front of a computer monitor. There was no one else there.

Jennifer looked up, saw Rhodes, and said, "Hot enough for you, Sheriff?"

Rhodes grinned. He could take a joke. Besides, he was going to be charming.

"You beat me to it," he said.

Jennifer wasn't in a mood to be charmed.

"You're here about my source," she said.

"Can we talk here?" Rhodes asked.

It was really a foolish question. The editor was in his office, and Nelson "Goober" Vance was nowhere to be seen. Vance had for a while been the paper's only reporter, covering sports, writing features and columns, and writing all the news articles that didn't come from some service. But Vance had gotten tired of doing it all and threatened to quit, which was why Jennifer had been hired.

Rhodes had a feeling that the paper had gotten more than it bargained for.

"Goober doesn't come in until later," Jennifer said. "He says that he can sleep late for the first time in his life now that he has a cub reporter working here."

"Cub?" Rhodes said. "More like a full-grown grizzly."

"You're just saying that to flatter me."

"Not exactly, but you're doing something here that nobody has done in Clearview in my lifetime."

"You mean that nobody's ever investigated anything. Well, all I can say is that it's about time somebody did."

"Probably," Rhodes said. "But sometimes investigations have those unintended consequences you hear about."

"You can't blame me for Grat Bilson's death," Jennifer said. "I didn't have a thing to do with that."

"Not directly, no, and maybe not even indirectly. That's what we need to talk about."

Jennifer didn't look as if she wanted to talk. She looked as if she wanted to give Rhodes a good whack on the nose.

So much for charm.

"Am I a suspect?" Jennifer said.

Rhodes started to give her the "everybody's a suspect" line, but he was afraid she might not take it the right way. He said, "Not unless you make yourself one. What I want to talk about is something else entirely. I want to talk about what you have on Jay Beaman."

"I can't tell you that."

"Yes, you can. This isn't about some newspaper story now. It's about a murder. And if it's Grat Bilson who's been killed, I need all the information I can get."

"Why don't you just talk to Beaman?"

"Do you think he'd tell me anything? Has he told *you* anything?"

"No," Jennifer said. "No to both questions. But you're the sheriff, not just some blond girl reporter."

"All the more reason he wouldn't talk to me," Rhodes said. "You can't arrest him. I can."

Jennifer opened her mouth, closed it, and said nothing for a few seconds. Then she said, "Oh, all right, I'll tell you. Let me get my notes."

Charm, Rhodes thought. Gets 'em every time.

11

When it came right down to it, Jennifer didn't want to stay in the newspaper office to talk after all.

"I worked hard to get this information together," she said. "I don't want anybody sneaking up on us and getting a look at it."

Rhodes didn't think anyone would sneak up on them, but Goober Vance might come in and get nosy. So Rhodes suggested that he and Jennifer go to his office in the courthouse.

Jennifer agreed, and she followed Rhodes in her own car. When she arrived, he bought two Dr Peppers from the machine and gave one to her.

"I didn't know you could get them in bottles any more," she said.

"You can't except for a few places," Rhodes said, though he didn't know of any others. "And this is one of them."

They went into his office. Jennifer sat in front of the desk, holding her Dr Pepper in one hand and a manila folder in the other. The folder had been locked in the bottom drawer of her desk at the newspaper building.

"I'd just as soon not give you the folder," she

said. "You can ask questions, and I'll use the notes to answer them."

Rhodes took a drink of Dr Pepper. He wanted a look at the actual notes, but maybe he could find out what he needed to know without it. On the other hand, maybe he couldn't. If that turned out to be the case, he could turn on the charm again.

"Okay," he said, "here's the first question. What do you have on Jay Beaman?"

"You'll have to be more specific."

She was worse than Hack and Lawton, Rhodes thought. He said, "Grat Bilson is probably dead. He told you some things about Beaman. I have to know them. What were they?"

"You don't have to get snippy. For one thing, Mr. Beaman was having an affair with Mrs. Bilson."

"Apparently everyone in town knows that," Rhodes said. "What else?"

"You'll notice I said *was*. The affair was over a while ago. Mr. Beaman had a new interest."

Hack would be sorry to hear that, since he preferred to be the first with all the news. It was too bad that Rhodes couldn't mention it to him.

"And who was the new interest?" Rhodes asked.

"I've never met her," Jennifer said.

"I might get snippy again if you don't be more forthcoming," Rhodes said. "How did you find out about this new interest?"

"Mr. Bilson told me about her. He found out about it by accident."

"How?"

Jennifer flipped a few pages of notes until she found what she was looking for.

"He went in to see Mr. Beaman one day, but Mr. Beaman wasn't in his office. Mr. Bilson just happened to look at the computer screen, and that's when he found out."

Rhodes could just imagine how much truth there was in that story. Bilson had probably gone into the deserted office on purpose, and he'd no doubt deliberately looked at the computer screen. He might even have done a little snooping in the files.

"Exactly what did he find out?" Rhodes asked.

"That Mr. Beaman was dating a convict," Jennifer said.

"Dating a convict? You might want to explain that one to me."

Jennifer smiled. "I'd be glad to. What do you know about janesinjail.com?"

Rhodes just looked at her. He didn't have any idea what she was talking about.

"Now you'll have to explain your explanation," he said.

"It's a Web site. I thought you might have heard of it."

Rhodes didn't have a lot of time to play around on the Internet.

"You were wrong," he said.

"It's an interesting site," Jennifer told him. "Female inmates from several states, including Texas, post their pictures and a little information about themselves. Of course they don't tell you why they're in the penitentiary." She looked down at her notes. "They say things like, 'sensitive, poetry-loving woman wants to meet a man who appreciates free verse.' And the pictures are sometimes years old. Some of them are pretty provocative. The pictures, that is, not the inmates. But you don't care about that."

Rhodes wasn't sure whether he cared or not. He'd heard that everything was available on the Internet, but he'd never expected anything like this.

"Somehow I don't think the Texas Department of Criminal Justice sponsors that page," he said.

"No. It's sponsored by an individual. If you want to get in touch with one of the women, you have to go through him."

"Who is he?"

"Nobody knows, at least not that I can find out about. You have to go through an e-mail address to get in touch with him. Or her. It could be a woman, for all I know. Anyway, whoever it is sells you the address of the inmate you're interested in, and you can become her pen pal. No pun intended."

"I'll bet," Rhodes said. "How much does the address cost?"

"Five dollars."

"Cheap enough," Rhodes said. "You have to admire the guy's entrepreneurial spirit. But there's a big difference in writing some woman who's behind bars and dating her. *Dating* was the word you used, wasn't it?"

"That's right. And that's what I meant. But I did use an incorrect word. I said he was dating a convict. I should have said that he was dating an ex-convict. Mr. Bilson said the woman had been released."

"Nobody's notified me of an ex-convict living in the county," Rhodes said.

"Her name's Linda Fenton. Here's her picture."

Jennifer reached into the folder and brought out a picture printed on plain white paper.

"I printed it from the Web site," Jennifer said. "What do you think?"

Rhodes looked at the picture. He couldn't tell much about it. The woman looked a little young for Beaman, who was in his fifties. She had a round face, big eyes, and blond hair. She was wearing tight blue jeans and a belt with a big round western buckle. She had on a T-shirt that was even tighter than the jeans.

"She looks a little young," Rhodes said.

"It's an old picture, one that was taken when she was living in the free world."

"She's a little flashy looking, too," Rhodes said. "I can't understand why a man like Jay Beaman would be dating a convict. Ex-convict, I mean."

"Mr. Bilson said that there's no accounting for taste."

"I didn't know Grat had such a way with words," Rhodes said.

"He also told me that Mr. Beaman liked to take chances. That's one of the reasons he dated Mrs. Bilson, for the thrill of doing something a little illicit. He also liked to go down to La Marque and gamble at the dog track. La Marque's close to Texas City, down by Galveston."

Rhodes told her that he knew where Texas City was, and La Marque, too, and handed her the picture.

"As for why you haven't been notified about her being in the county," Jennifer said, putting the picture back in the folder, "she might be living in another county. Or she might have given a false address."

It wouldn't be the first time, Rhodes thought. He said, "Even at that, there's no law against a man dating an ex-convict."

"It wouldn't look good at election time, though," Jennifer said. "And Mr. Bilson told me he was going to get the word out, even if I didn't print the story. Besides, there's more to it than that."

"And you found out about it."

"That's right."

"So are you going to help me out some more?"

"I suppose. But for a sheriff, you don't always

ask the right questions. You should have asked me what Linda was in the pen for."

"You said that wasn't on the Web site," Rhodes said.

"Sure. But anybody can find out what someone's in prison for. It's a public record."

"And you're a reporter."

"Is that a nice way of saying I'm a snoop?" Jennifer asked.

"No, it's a compliment. Not everyone would take the trouble to look it up."

"Well, I did."

"You're going to save me the trouble, I hope."

"I suppose so."

"Good. Tell me what she was in for."

"Arson," Jennifer said.

12

According to Jennifer Loam, Linda Fenton had been married, and she and her husband had owned a restaurant in Houston. It hadn't been doing well. In fact, it had been losing money, and her husband was getting ready to declare bankruptcy.

But then a miracle happened: the restaurant burned to the ground. Mr. Fenton had told people that it was probably an electrical fire, or maybe a grease fire, but the arson investigators found out that the fire had been deliberately set.

At first their suspicions settled on Mr. Fenton, which Jennifer told Rhodes was typically sexist.

"Not really," Rhodes said. "Most arsonists are men. I'd say more than 95 percent."

"Are you making that up?" Jennifer asked.

"No. I might not have exactly the right figure, but it's close enough."

"Oh," Jennifer said. "I suppose it wasn't sexist at all, then."

"It wasn't. Fenton was the natural suspect."

"Maybe." Jennifer didn't sound entirely convinced, but she went on to say that after the investigators had pretty much decided that Mr.

Fenton wasn't guilty, they went looking for disgruntled employees. There hadn't been any of those, however, and Linda Fenton had made a mistake. The newspapers weren't clear on precisely what it was, but it seemed to Rhodes from the way Jennifer told the story that Linda had probably talked to a friend and said a little too much.

Or maybe it was her husband she'd talked to. At any rate, someone told the police, and Linda Fenton was arrested, tried, and convicted.

There were other troubles in her past, including a couple of DWIs, during the course of which she'd assaulted an officer and resisted arrest. She'd had the bad luck of drawing a stern judge in the arson case, so she got a stiff penalty.

"And now she's out," Rhodes said when Jennifer had finished. "You did some good research."

"You don't have to butter me up."

"Just telling the truth," Rhodes said, thinking that sometimes when you were being charming, you just couldn't turn it off.

"Well, anyway, there's lots more," Jennifer said. "Mr. Beaman's been a pretty naughty commissioner."

"Let's have the rest of it, then," Rhodes said.

"This is where we get to the touchy part," Jennifer said. "The part that's hard to prove. It's also the criminal part."

"The good stuff," Rhodes said.

"Absolutely. I'm still developing it."

"But you're going to tell me about it anyway, right?"

"Yes. Maybe you can help me. There might not be a law against dating ex-convicts, but there's certainly one against bribery."

"Now we're getting to it," Rhodes said. "Who's bribed Beaman?"

Jennifer couldn't prove that anyone had. But there was a big road project coming up, the complete renovation and repair of one of the county roads. The road passed through Beaman's precinct.

"I know all about that," Rhodes said. "People have been complaining about that road for years. It's about time something was done. I don't see what that has to do with a bribe, though."

"Do you know who got the contract for the road?"

"I believe it was Ralph Oliver."

"That's right. And do you know how contractors for road projects are selected?"

Rhodes knew, all right. It was a bit of a sore point with some people. The way it worked was simple. There was no bidding system. The commissioners got to choose the contractor. They could pick anyone they wanted, and then the county engineer had to negotiate the price.

"Ralph made a huge campaign contribution to Beaman last year," Jennifer said.

"That doesn't prove anything," Rhodes told her.

"No. The commissioners always argue that their friends give them campaign contributions and that it's only logical that they would choose their friends for county projects. After all, they know them and trust them, so why not reward them?"

"It makes sense if you look at it like that," Rhodes said.

"Only if you trust the commissioners. What if they award contracts only to the people who give them the most money? Isn't that a bribe?"

"Not necessarily."

"Maybe not. But how much money do you think Beaman spent on his last campaign?"

"Probably not much. He didn't even have an opponent."

"That's right," Jennifer said. "He printed up a few signs, nailed them to fence posts, and that was it."

"All right. I believe you. So what?"

"So nothing. If that was all there was to it, then there'd be no harm done, except that Beaman would have a big campaign chest that wasn't being used. As it is, though, I think he used it. That's what I'm trying to prove."

"It's his. He can use it."

"Not to build his own road," Jennifer said. "Not to have a stock tank dug on his property."

"No," Rhodes said. "He can't do that."

"He's not supposed to use county equipment, either, but he did," Jennifer said. "At least I think he did. I'm still working on that, too."

Rhodes thought that she must be going after the Pulitzer.

"That's going to ruin him if it's true," he said. "Get him indicted, too."

"That's right. Someone might kill to keep from going to prison."

"Maybe he killed the wrong person," Rhodes said.

Jennifer frowned. Then her lips slowly curled into a smile, and she laughed.

"You had me going for just a second there. I'm no threat to him if I don't have the evidence, and my informant seems to be dead."

"I'm still not a hundred percent sure of that," Rhodes said.

"I think he is, but I'm not going to stop digging. Now that I'm on the trial, I'll find out if what I've been told is true."

"Beaman isn't stupid," Rhodes said. "He might act like a hick, call you 'little lady,' and pat you on the head, but he's been in office a long time. He's shrewd."

"He's dating an ex-convict that he met on the Internet. How shrewd is that?"

"Not very," Rhodes said. "But you're going to need some help with this."

"Are you offering?"

"No," Rhodes said. "Not yet. I have a body to deal with. Maybe you can find another informant. And besides, you're not even sure Bilson was telling you the truth. Remember, he told you that I was cheating the county, too. It was easy to prove I wasn't."

"You're right," Jennifer said. "It was easy. I checked."

"I thought you might. Have you checked all these other stories?"

"I told you that I was working on it."

"But you haven't proved anything yet."

"Not yet, but I will. It won't be as easy without Mr. Bilson's help, though. I have a feeling everything's pretty well hidden."

"You can bet on it," Rhodes said. "If there's anything to be hidden, that is."

"I know there is. He couldn't have made all that stuff up."

"He might not have made it up, but he could have been wrong."

"I don't think so."

"Which means you're putting all your faith in what Grat Bilson told you. Is that right?"

Jennifer got a stubborn look. "He knows what he's talking about. Or knew."

"He didn't know about me. He was dead wrong about that."

"I'll admit that bothers me. That's why I'm going to be absolutely sure before I publish anything."

"Your editor will make sure you're more than sure," Rhodes said, and Jennifer grimaced.

Then the phone on the desk rang twice in

quick succession. A double ring meant that Hack was calling from the jail.

"I'll have to answer that," Rhodes said.

Jennifer shrugged as if to say she didn't mind, and Rhodes picked up the phone.

"You know that fireworks stand out toward Milsby?" Hack asked when Rhodes answered.

"I was by there yesterday."

"Well, you better get by there again. Someone called in on a cell phone, said he'd been there tryin' to buy some fireworks when a crazy woman came up with a gun and threatened to blow the place all to hell and gone."

"I'm leaving right now," Rhodes said.

"If you hear a real loud noise," Hack said, "you'll know you're too late."

13

The county car rumbled down the gravel-topped road, raising a rooster tail of dust that drifted out over the dry fields as Rhodes passed them. The dust was also coating the two-door Saturn that followed along behind him, the one being driven by Jennifer Loam.

Rhodes had tried to tell her not to come, but while he knew she hadn't heard what Hack had said, she could tell from Rhodes's response that something was going on. Nothing Rhodes said had persuaded her to stay behind, not that he'd been able to say much. He'd been in too much of a hurry to get to his car.

He pulled into the bare-dirt parking lot of the fireworks stand, and as he stepped out of the car, all the dust that had been following him caught up and swirled around him. Then Jennifer drove up beside him, and even more dust surged over him. He could feel grit under his eyelids, and he tried to blink it away.

He blinked again, and his watering eyes could see two people inside the stand. They were a couple of feet apart, and he could hear them yelling at each other. The dust rolled on over the fireworks stand, but it didn't seem to bother the people inside it. Rhodes didn't think they even noticed.

"What's happening?" Jennifer asked, coming to stand beside him.

"That's what I'm here to find out," he said. "And you'd better stay in your car. You don't want to interfere with an officer in the performance of his duties. You don't want to get shot, either, I'll bet."

"Who are they?" she asked. "Who has the gun?"

"I don't know," Rhodes said. He was tired of being charming. "I can't see well enough to be sure. Now get in your car."

He half expected an argument, but Jennifer didn't say a word. She turned and walked back to her little car and got inside.

Rhodes turned back to the fireworks stand. His vision had cleared, and he understood at once why Jennifer hadn't given him any argument.

One of the women was Yvonne Bilson, and she had a pistol in her right hand. She was waving it around and screaming.

"You dirty bitch! I don't care if it kills me along with you. I'm going to blow you to kingdom come."

Rhodes didn't take the threat very seriously. He figured that if Yvonne had really intended to blow anything or anybody up, she'd have done it by now. She'd had plenty of time. It had taken him at least ten minutes to get there.

On the other hand, it might not matter what she intended. She could always accomplish her threat by accident.

"I never took anybody away from you," the fireworks salesperson said. "He wasn't yours in the first place. You were living in adultery."

It finally dawned on Rhodes that the salesperson was a woman. He hadn't been able to see her clearly when he'd passed by the stand on the way to and from the place where Bilson had died, but now that he could, he thought she looked familiar.

"Don't tell me about adultery, you whore," Yvonne said. She pointed the pistol at a display of Roman candles. "We'll see how you like having fire up your ass."

Rhodes thought it was about time for him to do something, so he walked forward and said, "Put down the gun, Yvonne."

Yvonne didn't turn to see who was talking to her, but she knew who he was. She said, "Don't tell me what to do, you son of a bitch. If you'd just done your job, none of this would ever have happened."

"What job is that?" Rhodes asked.

"Arresting people," Yvonne said, still not taking her eyes off the other woman.

"It's not against the law to sell fireworks," Rhodes said. "I know Grat was working on that, but —"

"I'm not talking about selling fireworks, you dumb son of a bitch. I'm talking about letting

105

convicts roam around the county as free as the air."

Rhodes recognized the other woman then. Linda Fenton. She was older than she'd been in the picture he'd seen, but her face hadn't changed much. She was still blond, and she still liked to wear tight jeans.

"She's not a convict," Rhodes said. "She's been released."

"I don't see what difference that makes."

"You've never been behind bars, have you, honey," Linda said.

She had a deep, husky voice that sounded to Rhodes like the voice of someone who'd smoked a lot of cigarettes, though he knew that smoking had been prohibited in Texas prisons for years.

"No," Yvonne said. "I've never been in the pen. I'm not a convict like you."

"If you don't put down that gun, you're gonna be," Linda said.

Yvonne said that she didn't care. "You took my boyfriend and my husband. So whatever happens to me now doesn't matter."

"It'll matter once you get behind them bars," Linda told her. "It's not as nice there as you think it is."

Sweat was running down Rhodes's face and mixing with all the dust that had settled there. He wondered what the temperature was. Probably over a hundred. He looked at the ground around the fireworks stand. Where he was standing was completely bare of grass, as was most of the area in front of the stand, and what grass there was nearby was so short and close to the ground that it couldn't possibly catch on fire no matter what happened.

But about ten feet behind the stand there was a barbed-wire fence, and behind the fence was a thick growth of johnsongrass, most of it already burned brown by the sun. Just a little spark would set it afire, and the blaze would spread quickly all over the field and maybe beyond.

"It's not just what happens to you, Yvonne," Rhodes said. "If you set that field on fire, you're likely to cause some real trouble. This place is so dry that the fire could spread all the way to Milsby."

"Wouldn't be any great loss if the whole damn place went up in smoke," Yvonne said. "Nothing left of it anyway. Besides, it wouldn't matter to me, not if I was down in Huntsville in the big house."

"We don't call it the big house, honey," Linda said.

Rhodes thought she was taking the whole thing very calmly, especially since Yvonne still had the pistol pointed at the Roman candles.

That was probably better than having the pistol pointed at the firecrackers, Rhodes thought.

In his misspent childhood, in the days when fireworks were legal everywhere and when even little kids played with them all the time, Rhodes had more than once pulled the fuse out of a firecracker, set the remaining little tube down on the sidewalk, and clobbered it with a hammer just to see what would happen. More often than not, the resulting explosions had been more than satisfactory. A bullet would have a lot more impact than a hammer, and the chain reaction it might start was something Rhodes preferred not to think about.

If the impact of the bullet didn't set things off, there was always the muzzle flash. The end of the pistol barrel wasn't more than a few inches from the firecrackers, easily within range of the flash if she pulled the trigger.

"I don't care whether you call it the big house or the Graybar Hotel," Yvonne said. "Doesn't make a damn bit of difference to me."

"And it's not at Huntsville, either," Linda said. "You'd be stuck out in Gatesville or some-where. That dry weather out that way's really bad on your skin."

"Wouldn't matter a whole lot, would it?" Yvonne said. "Not if I was locked up with a bunch of women. It'd be worth it, anyway, if the world was rid of you."

Rhodes walked a few steps closer to the stand. The shelves behind the women were filled with fireworks wrapped in crinkly paper printed in bright red, yellow, blue, and shiny black. On one shelf there were stacks of black cat rockets, along with other bottle rockets and ten-ball Roman candles, some of them the whistling kind. Boxes of sparklers were stacked beside them. Above those items there were shelves filled with fountains and cones with names like Apache Firedance, Barracuda, Gargantua, and California Condor. Beside the fountains were some helicopters and airplane-shaped items, along with spinning disks. And there were fire-crackers, lots of firecrackers, in all sizes: thunder bombs, silver salutes, M-80s, cherry bombs, black cats, and wolf packs.

It occurred to Rhodes that if everything went off all at once, there wouldn't be just a fire. There would be a mushroom cloud over Blacklin County to rival those he used to see in the old black-and-white science fiction movies he watched on TV.

And there would be a great big crater right about where he was standing. It wasn't an appealing prospect, but Rhodes wasn't especially worried. People who talked as much as Yvonne was talking didn't generally shoot anyone. After they'd let off enough steam, they were ready to forgive and forget and move on to something else.

"Yvonne," he said, "you're wrong about this whole thing. Ms. Fenton didn't do anything, and we're not even sure that Grat's dead. We talked about that, remember?"

Yvonne kept her eyes on Linda Fenton when she spoke. "I remember. But Grat's still missing, and there's a dead body at the funeral parlor. This bitch here's the one who did it, too. She likes to play with fire."

"What about your husband's girlfriend?" Linda asked.

"You better shut your mouth about that," Yvonne said. "Grat didn't like anybody but me."

Rhodes was interested in hearing what Linda had to say. He hadn't known about any girlfriend, and neither had Hack. For that matter, Hack didn't seem to have known about Linda Fenton, either. It wasn't usual for Hack to be so far out of the loop. Rhodes would have to ask him about that, if he ever got the chance. Yvonne was getting worked up again.

"I don't know why you think he didn't have a girlfriend," Linda said. "After all, you were runnin' around on him with half the men in the county."

"You better stop talking like that about me," Yvonne said. "I'm going to blow the both of us up if you don't."

With that, she stopped pointing the pistol at the Roman candles. She moved it up in line with the firecrackers.

Rhodes didn't like the way things were going. He risked walking up to the fireworks stand until he was standing in the scant shade of the canopy. It was still hot, but at least the sun wasn't burning a hole in the top of his head.

"Why don't you just give me the pistol, Yvonne," he said. "We can talk this over a lot better without that gun being in the way."

"I don't think so," Yvonne said. "And I'm

tired of talking, anyway. This bitch has started lying about Grat."

She looked at all the firecrackers, smiled, and said, "I wonder what'll happen when I pull the trigger?"

"You don't really want to find out," Rhodes said.

"Oh yes I do," Yvonne said, and fired the pistol.

14

Rhodes hit the dirt and rolled under the plywood counter that jutted out from the front of the fireworks stand. From where he was lying, he couldn't really see everything that happened, but he could see quite a bit more than he wanted to. And he could hear it all.

There were explosions, of course. Lots of them. They started with a string of firecrackers going off. After that everything ran together, *pop-pop-pop-pop,* like the .22 shots that Hack had described, only in far greater numbers. Through their rapid reports Rhodes could distinguish the much noisier blasts of the M-80s, the cherry bombs, and the larger silver salutes. He'd never been in a foxhole during wartime, but he thought the sound might be something like what he was experiencing now.

Besides the firecrackers and the bigger, louder devices, he could hear the keening of the rockets as they took off in a straight line over the counter and whistled toward the road before exploding. Rhodes hoped that Jennifer had stayed in her car.

The helicopters and spinning disks went off in all directions, gyrating and revolving as they made whirring and buzzing sounds. Some of them wobbled across the parking lot, pinged off the hood and roof of the county car, and landed on the ground, where they kept right on rotating madly, as if attempting to drill a hole in the hard-packed dirt.

The volcanoes and cones were spewing colors and noise, and balls of fire were bouncing off the underside of the roof of the stand and falling back down. Rhodes was all right under the counter, but he didn't know about Linda Fenton and Yvonne on the other side. He thought for a second about getting up, but there was a whooping sound like a thousand tiny mortars firing, and the Roman candles started to discharge colored balls of flame that flew out toward the road and bounced around on the dirt and gravel.

Rhodes had to admit that it was a spectacular sight, even from his vantage point. Even in the daylight. There were explosions of every color of the rainbow: red, orange, yellow, green, blue, indigo, and violet. Well, maybe no indigo and violet, but plenty of the others.

All the burned powder smelled like the aftermath of a gun battle, and Rhodes could smell something else, too. The fireworks stand was burning.

Rhodes didn't much feel like standing up, since the fireworks were still detonating fairly rapidly, but he supposed he didn't have a choice. He had to see if Linda and Yvonne were all right.

He rolled forward, stood up, and eased his head above the counter. Sparklers were fizzing and sputtering brilliantly, but Rhodes didn't have time to admire them. A Roman candle ball nearly took out his right eye, and a rocket whizzed by his left shoulder pulling a tail of sparks behind it. He ducked back down and waited a few seconds longer while the volcanoes erupted, the candles shot fire, the rockets glared red, and the firecrackers popped and blasted.

Finally things seemed to get a bit quieter. Rhodes wasn't sure whether it was just his imagination or whether his hearing was permanently damaged, but he decided to take another look.

The sparklers had about fizzled out, and there were only a few random bursts of noise. To Rhodes's surprise, there were still quite a few unexploded fireworks left on the shelves. He'd thought the entire contents of the stand had gone off, but only a couple of feet were missing.

Yvonne and Linda were huddled facedown on the ground, their hands over their heads. The roof of the stand was burning. Linda Fenton wasn't moving, and neither was Yvonne. Rhodes couldn't see the pistol.

He turned to look for Jennifer. The reporter was sitting in her car with her cell phone at her ear. She waved with her free hand to let Rhodes know she was all right.

The back of the stand was open behind the shelves, and some of the fireworks had gone out that way. Not many, but enough to set the dead johnsongrass on fire. Rhodes hoped Jennifer was calling the fire department instead of trying to find a wire service that wanted a story about the big explosion in Blacklin County.

He walked around the end of the counter to check on the two women. Linda Fenton sat up and looked around. The backs of her shirt and pants were scorched, but she seemed all right otherwise.

"What the hell happened?" she said, or something like that. Rhodes wasn't quite sure. His ears still weren't working properly.

Yvonne Bilson didn't say a word, not that Rhodes could hear. She just jumped up and started running toward the burning field. Rhodes didn't think she'd get far, but she surprised him. She went through the barbed-wire fence as if she'd been practicing for the back-country Olympics and took off through the blazing grass like it wasn't even on fire.

Rhodes considered yelling, "Stop, or I'll shoot!" but he knew Yvonne wouldn't stop, even if she could hear him, which he doubted, so there was nothing he could do but go after her.

He didn't get through the fence nearly as quickly as Yvonne had. He'd never been extremely agile, and the barbs snagged first in the back of his shirt and then on the leg of his pants. He finally got through, but he knew the rip in his shirt couldn't be repaired. He could probably save the pants, however.

Running through a grassfire on a hot day

wasn't Rhodes's idea of a good time. The fire hadn't really gotten started good, but Rhodes still felt as if the soles of his shoes were burning, and he was sure he didn't have to worry about the snag in the shirt any longer. It was going to be burned and scorched so much that no one would ever notice the rip. He slapped at a spark that landed on the pocket.

The acrid smoke was biting into Rhodes's lungs with every breath, and he knew that before long there would be a dark gray tower that could be seen from most parts of the county.

Rhodes ran out of the fire quickly, but it was following right along behind him as surely as he was following Yvonne. He was moving faster than the fire, because luckily enough there wasn't much wind to spread it. Maybe it wouldn't get to the trees before the fire trucks got there. Assuming that Jennifer had called for them.

Yvonne was going to get to the trees, however. Rhodes would never have thought she could run so fast. He thought that smoking was supposed to be bad for the lungs, but Yvonne smoked a lot, and it didn't seem to have had any effect on her. Of course with all the smoke he'd inhaled as he ran, he might as well have smoked a pack a day for the past year or so.

Maybe, he thought, it wasn't that Yvonne was running fast so much as that he was running slowly. Either way, she was gaining on him. The problem wasn't the fire now. It was the grass, which was thick and high and hard to run through. Even though it was mostly dead, it slashed at Rhodes's hands and arms, and occasionally even at his face.

Just as Yvonne got to the edge of the trees she stopped. Rhodes thought for a second that she was out of breath, and he felt a little surge of pride to think that he wasn't really breathing so hard himself. No harder than if he'd run about ten hundred-yard dashes back-to-back while carrying a refrigerator on his shoulders.

But Yvonne wasn't out of breath, and Rhodes learned where the pistol was.

She still had it, and it was in her hand.

And now she was shooting at him.

Rhodes didn't actually hear the shot, but he saw a puff of smoke from the pistol barrel. He had no idea where the bullet went. All he knew was that it didn't hit him, so he kept on going.

Yvonne fired again, but that shot didn't hit Rhodes either. Yvonne said something, or Rhodes thought she did. He could see her mouth move. Probably something involving "son of a bitch," Rhodes thought.

Yvonne didn't say anything else. She turned and ran for the trees. She was into them quickly, but Rhodes wasn't as far behind as he had been. He'd managed to gain a little ground while she was shooting at him.

When he got to the trees, he stopped for a second. It wouldn't do to go rushing right into the little woods. It wasn't that he needed to catch his breath, he told himself. He was stopping for safety reasons. He had to be careful. For all he knew Yvonne wasn't any more than ten feet away, hiding behind the trunk of some patchy old elm or hickory nut tree, just waiting for him.

He looked back over his shoulder. The fire was still spreading but not rapidly. The smoke was floating lazily upward, and Rhodes thought he could see a billow of dust on the country road that might mean the fire trucks were on the way. If so, he'd have to thank Jennifer for her quick thinking.

He turned back to the trees. His breathing wasn't so ragged now, and his lungs weren't burning so much from the smoke.

Rhodes wondered how far the woods extended. Most of the land in this part of the county had been cleared long ago, and it was unlikely that there were woods of any size left. Yvonne had entered the woods at about the midpoint, and they extended for about a quarter of a mile in either direction. They probably weren't more than a quarter of a mile deep, either, certainly no more than a half. Unfortunately that meant there were plenty of hiding places.

"Yvonne," Rhodes called out. His voice sounded hollow and strange in his ears. "Are you in there?"

There was no answer. Or maybe there was, and he just couldn't hear it. He pulled out his own pistol and started into the trees.

15

Rhodes didn't hear the shot this time, either, but it whacked the bark off a tree near his right cheek, and he felt the sting as the chips of wood hit his face, narrowly missing his right eye. First the rocket, now the wood chips. Rhodes figured that the way things were going, he'd be lucky if he got home with both eyes intact.

He squatted down, but Yvonne didn't fire again. He wondered if she was counting her shots. He was. She'd fired four, and she'd been carrying what looked like a .32-caliber Smith & Wesson revolver, the regulation police model with a three-inch barrel. It had probably belonged to Grat, not that it mattered. What mattered was how many cartridges were in the chambers. The pistol held six. Had Yvonne (or Grat, whoever had loaded it) left an empty chamber under the hammer? There was no way of knowing at the moment. What Rhodes did know was that Yvonne had either one or two shots left. So far she hadn't proved to be accurate enough to scare him, but you never knew when a poor shot might get lucky. Even a blind hog rooted up an acorn now and then, as Dan Rather might say in the heat of presidential election coverage.

Not only did Rhodes not want to get shot himself, he didn't want to have to shoot Yvonne. He didn't like shooting people, especially people like Yvonne, who were grief-stricken and didn't really know what they were doing. He'd seldom been forced to shoot anyone in his career as sheriff, and he was glad of it. Still, he kept his pistol in his hand. Maybe it would scare Yvonne, though Rhodes didn't think that anything would scare her, not while she was in her current state of mind.

It was much cooler in the trees than in the field, thanks both to the shade and to the fact that the fire was still a hundred yards or more away. Rhodes couldn't hear any birds or animals, but that didn't mean they weren't there. There was no breeze at all to stir the leaves or to cool the sweat on Rhodes's face.

Rhodes stood up, careful to keep the trunk of a tree between himself and where he thought Yvonne might be. He turned and looked back across the field and saw the pumper trucks from the fire department pulling up beside the fireworks stand. He hoped they'd get the fire under control quickly.

He tried to think about where Yvonne might be. She could be hiding or she could be running. He couldn't hear her even if she was making a lot of noise, thanks to the ringing in his ears. He decided that running was probably the more likely option for her to choose. She hadn't waited around for anything at the fireworks stand. Rhodes started walking, looking to his left and right, hoping that he would see Yvonne before she saw him, assuming she was still around to see him.

The sunlight that filtered down through the trees was just as hot as it had been out in the field, and Rhodes wished he had a drink of cool water to soothe his scratchy throat. He brushed his left hand across his sweaty face and looked at his fingers. They were dark with soot and dirt.

If Rhodes had been an expert woodsman, he might have been able to track Yvonne, but he wasn't an expert. He could read obvious signs, like torn cloth stuck to a tree branch, and he could tell if someone had broken a limb off a bush, but that was about the extent of his skills. There was no piece of cloth anywhere, and there were no broken branches, so Rhodes had to hope that Yvonne would make some kind of mistake and lead him to her.

She didn't. Rhodes came out of the trees without finding her, and walked into an open field. There was no sign of Yvonne anywhere. There was nothing but a stock tank with a low earthen dam and a few cattle grazing nearby, or trying to. This field had been kept clear. There was hardly any grass for the cattle to eat, and there was no place for Yvonne to have hidden herself. Rhodes thought she must still be in the woods. She'd gone sideways instead of through.

He started to head back to the trees when he

thought he'd better check the tank. There was a chance that Yvonne might be hunkered down on the other side of the dam.

Rhodes couldn't decide whether to walk around to one side of the dam or to go up over the top. There was a scraggly little willow tree on top, just about dead from lack of water. Its leaves were a sickly yellow, and quite a few of them were lying on top of the dirt around the bottom of the tree. As scrawny as the tree was, however, it would provide a bit of cover, so Rhodes thought he might as well go that way.

The dam wasn't too steep, and Rhodes climbed it easily. He walked up behind the willow and eased his way through the sparse leaves until he could see the other side of the dam.

The little stock tank was nearly dry. The water had receded to a hole in the middle of where the tank had once been, and all around there was thick, cracked mud, dry on top but sloppy underneath. It was broken by trails the cattle had made as they went for a drink. Rhodes thought it was lucky that none of them had gotten mired down.

There was no sign of Yvonne, but there was a row of little bushes that stood down where the waterline had once been. She might be hidden behind one of them. Rhodes tried to get a little closer and have a look without leaving the partial concealment of the willow tree.

As he got near the edge of the dam, Yvonne

popped up from behind a bush and fired the pistol at him again. She didn't hit a vital spot, but the bullet took the heel off his left shoe, and Rhodes fell heavily. He hit the dam and rolled down the side, headed right for the bush where Yvonne was waiting.

Rhodes's hands were both empty. He had lost his pistol and had no idea where it was. There wasn't anything he could do about that, so he tried to make the best of things. He managed to keep rolling and to shift himself just enough so that he rolled past the bush instead of hitting it. When he passed it, he reached out and grabbed Yvonne's ankles, pulling her down with him.

They tumbled out onto the caked mud, and Yvonne kicked Rhodes in the face. Then she crawled toward the bank.

Rhodes grabbed her ankle and pulled her back. She hit him on the side of the head with the pistol.

Well, he thought, *I guess that means it's empty.*

He didn't let go of the ankle, so Yvonne hit him again.

He let go.

Yvonne fell backward and sat down hard on the mud, breaking through the crust and sinking an inch or two into the goop beneath. She jumped up and her foot went through the crust. This time she fell forward, and she put out her hands to catch herself. It worked in that she didn't land on her face, but her hands both went

123

down into the mud, and when they came out, she wasn't holding the pistol.

Rhodes started crawling toward her as she dug down into the sludge, trying to find the gun. Maybe it wasn't empty after all. Or maybe Yvonne just wasn't sure.

Rhodes gathered himself, froglike, and launched himself toward her. He got his arms around her, and they rolled away from the place where the gun was sunk in the mud. As they rolled, Yvonne kicked and struggled. They broke through the sun-baked rind in several places, and soon they were sliding instead of rolling, coated with the slick mud that not too long before had been on the bottom of the tank. Yvonne was splattering mud everywhere with her struggles. It smelled old and foul, almost as if it had been part of a hog pen instead of a stock tank.

Rhodes's hearing was getting a little better, because he was pretty sure he could hear Yvonne cursing him and calling him a son of a bitch.

He was trying to hold on to her, but she was so slick with mud that it was like trying to hold a greased eel. Before he knew it, she had slipped away and was squirming back to where she'd lost the pistol. Rhodes didn't want her to shoot him or hit him again. His head was still throbbing from the last time. He staggered to his feet and went after her.

He didn't get far. The mud was too slick, and

he slipped down. He sat and watched helplessly as Yvonne pulled the mud-coated pistol up and pointed it at him.

She was quite a sight, kneeling there. There was mud smeared all over her clothes and face, and it was stuck in her hair as well. Rhodes was sure he didn't look any better. It would be a shame, he thought, to get shot and killed while looking like a man made out of mud. Clyde Ballinger would have his work cut out for him to get the corpse cleaned up and ready for viewing.

Except that it wasn't Rhodes who'd be killed if the gun went off.

"You'd better not pull that trigger, Yvonne," Rhodes said. "That gun barrel's full of mud. The pistol will just explode and take your hand off. Maybe your whole arm."

"You son of a bitch," Yvonne said.

"Just put down the pistol," Rhodes told her. "You don't want to hurt me, or yourself either."

"You don't know what I want."

Rhodes had to admit that he didn't, but he didn't say so. He stood up carefully, stuck out his hand, and said, "Give me the pistol."

"You can go to hell."

Rhodes took a slow step toward her.

"I'll help you up," Rhodes said. "But give me the gun first. You don't want to hurt anybody."

Yvonne shook her head, and Rhodes didn't know whether she understood him or not.

It didn't much matter if she did. She pulled the trigger anyway.

16

Nothing happened.

Yvonne had fired the last bullet earlier, after all, and now the gun was empty.

Rhodes took a deep breath and let it out slowly. He walked carefully over to Yvonne and held out his hand. She put the pistol in it, and Rhodes stuck the gun in his belt.

"We'd better be getting back to see what's happening with the fire," Rhodes said.

"Don't give a damn," Yvonne said. "You gonna put me in jail?"

"Well," Rhodes said, "let me see. You've assaulted a police officer, attempted to murder him, tried to blow up a fireworks stand, set a grass fire, unlawfully possessed a deadly weapon, and recklessly endangered me and Linda Fenton. Did I leave anything out?"

"Yeah, you son of a bitch. You left out abusive language."

"Right," Rhodes said. "I think you made some terroristic threats, too, but I'm willing to forget those."

"Does that mean you won't lock me up?"

"No," Rhodes said. "It doesn't mean I won't lock you up."

"Damn. I don't want to be a convict. That'll make me no better than that whore Fenton."

"Don't worry about it," Rhodes said. "That's the least of your problems. Let's go."

They started up over the dam, and Rhodes located his pistol. He was glad he saw it before Yvonne did, not that she seemed inclined to violence any longer. He picked the pistol up and held it well away from her.

"Be careful," he said when they started down the side of the dam. "I wouldn't want you to fall and hurt yourself."

Yvonne laughed. "Don't worry, Sheriff. I'll be careful."

After they came out of the trees, they had to walk around the grass fire, which was just about extinguished. A large area of the field was completely blackened, but there were no flames that Rhodes could see. The pumper trucks had things pretty much under control. Rhodes didn't see Chief Parker anywhere, but he waved at Trace Newman, who was too busy hanging on to a hose and spraying water to wave back.

Jennifer Loam was waiting when they got back to the fireworks stand, but Linda Fenton was nowhere around.

"She left," Jennifer said. "There was an old pickup parked over there, and I guess it was hers."

"Probably Jay Beaman's," Yvonne said. "Cons don't have trucks."

"She wasn't a con," Rhodes said.

"Same thing as one, then."

"You two look like you've been making mud pies," Jennifer said.

Rhodes said he thought it was more likely they looked like they'd been working as extras in a remake of *Creature from the Black Lagoon*.

"What's that?" Jennifer said. "A movie?"

"Never mind," Rhodes said. He had a tendency to forget that most people Jennifer's age had never seen a black-and-white movie, even on television. "Thanks for calling the fire department."

"I thought I'd better. You looked too busy to do it yourself."

"Well, I appreciate it. I think the fire's contained since there was no wind. We got lucky."

Rhodes could feel the mud hardening on him. He was going to be encased in a hard shell like an M&M, except that his shell wouldn't be made of candy.

"Are you going to take Ms. Bilson to the jail?" Jennifer asked.

"That's right," Rhodes said.

"Would it be all right if I interviewed her?"

"Here?"

"No. In the jail. After she gets cleaned up."

"I'll think about it," Rhodes said.

"I'm not talking to anybody," Yvonne said. "I'm not saying another word to anybody."

"You heard what she said," Rhodes told Jennifer.

"I'm coming by anyway," Jennifer said to Yvonne. "Maybe you'll change your mind."

"Not likely."

"I have to go write a story now," Jennifer said. "I'll see you later."

"Won't do you any good," Yvonne said, but Jennifer didn't reply. She got in her car and drove away.

That was all right with Rhodes. He didn't particularly want an interview with Yvonne appearing in the local paper. He touched her elbow and guided her to the county car. When they got there, he saw that the hood and top had been dented and scorched by the helicopters and Roman candles.

Yvonne saw what he was looking at and said, "I know what you're thinking."

Rhodes gave her a skeptical glance.

"Damaging county property," Yvonne said. "That's what you're thinking. Go ahead and add it to that list of charges you're making out. See if I care."

"I thought you weren't going to talk to anybody."

"I meant reporters. I'll talk to you, but I'm not talking to any reporters."

"All right," Rhodes said. He opened the back door of the car. "You can get in now. Watch your head."

Yvonne got inside, and Rhodes shut the door.

As he drove back to Clearview, he got Hack

on the radio and told him to get Ruth Grady to the jail.

"What for?" Hack asked.

"Never mind. Just have her there."

"Yes, sir, Mr. Sheriff, sir. You're the boss. I'm just the hired help. You give the orders, and I follow 'em. I don't need a reason. That's the natural order of things."

"I'll be there in ten minutes," Rhodes said.

"Great gobs of goose grease!" Hack said when Rhodes and Yvonne came in through the jail door. "I wish Lawton was here. He ain't ever gonna believe this when I tell him about it. You two look like you've been in a mud-rasslin' contest."

"We have," Rhodes said. "Is Ruth here?"

" 'Course she is. You told me to get her, didn't you?"

"Then where is she?"

"Well, I didn't mean she was *here*, exactly. But she's on the way. She was down in Thurston. It'll take her a few more minutes. I can see why you needed her, though. What on earth happened?"

"I'll tell you later," Rhodes said, feeling good about being one up on Hack for a change.

Hack would have had something more to say about it, but Ruth Grady came in. She stood looking at Rhodes and Yvonne for a second. Then she said, "When I was a little girl, I used to read this comic book called *Swamp Thing*."

Rhodes said, "I saw the movie. Adrienne

Barbeau and Louis Jourdan. But I was thinking more along the lines of *Creature from the Black Lagoon*."

"What's that?" Ruth asked.

Rhodes sighed and said, "Never mind. I want you to take charge of the prisoner, get her booked and cleaned up. In that order."

"Yes, sir," Ruth said.

"When you do that, there's somebody I'd like for you to go looking for."

"Yes, sir," Ruth said.

The bottom of the bathtub looked like someone had dumped a sack of potting soil into it. Rhodes hoped he didn't clog up the pipes by washing all that dirt into the town's sewer system. He turned the spray from the shower on it and watched it streak off the porcelain and wash down the drain. He felt a little bit guilty about having used so much water, but he'd needed it to get clean, and now he needed more to be sure the tub could be used again.

Rhodes felt considerably better now that he'd taken a bath. He was clean, and he was even cool, having soaked in the water for a while. He'd also turned the air-conditioning down a notch or two. He'd have to remember to turn it up again before he left.

He looked at his face in the bathroom mirror. There was a little scratch where the tree bark had hit him, but otherwise he looked pretty much the same as always. He finished drying his hair with the towel and looked around for a comb. Ivy was always after him to use the hair dryer, but he preferred the towel. He found that as his hair thinned out, he could dry it quite quickly without electrical aid, proving, he supposed, that there were advantages to all kinds of things if you just looked at them in the right way.

There was a scale in the bathroom, conveniently located near the tub so you could weigh yourself on it either before or after your bath. Or both, if you wanted to.

Rhodes didn't want to. Ivy weighed now and then, but her weight never seemed to vary more than a few ounces one way or the other. Rhodes didn't weigh. It was a matter of principle with him. Or that was what he told Ivy if she asked. The truth was, he just didn't want to know his weight or how much it might vary.

After he was dressed, Rhodes went into the kitchen to see if there was anything in the refrigerator besides the tofu bologna and tofu cheese that Ivy thought was good for him.

There wasn't anything he wanted, however. Not even an old moldy piece of real cheese. He thought about going to the Bluebonnet for a hamburger, but he needed to get back to the jail. So he ate a sandwich with the fake stuff. It was okay, he supposed, though a good, greasy hamburger would have been a lot better. Some fried onion rings wouldn't have hurt, either.

No wonder I stay away from that scale, he thought.

Yvonne was sitting on the bunk in her cell. She looked much better than she had the last time Rhodes had seen her, even though her hair was still damp and hanging down in straight clumps and the jail-issue jumpsuit didn't really fit her very well.

"Linda Fenton said something at the fireworks stand that I wanted to ask you about," Rhodes said. "Something about Grat having a girlfriend."

"That son of a bitch."

"Never mind his ancestry. Let's talk about the girlfriend. Who is she?"

"I don't want to talk about her."

"It might help me find out who killed Grat."

"You said he might not be dead."

"He might be. He probably is. You know that."

"Yeah, I guess I do."

"So tell me who the girlfriend is."

"Vernell Lindsey," Yvonne said. "That whore."

17

Vernell Lindsey came to the door wearing a T-shirt that said *Famous Novelist* on the front in big red letters. Rhodes figured the shirt was intended ironically, though her romance novels had been fairly successful, or so he'd heard. The writers' conference she'd recently sponsored hadn't turned out so well, however.

"What do you want?" Vernell said, taking a puff from the cigarette she held in one hand.

"To talk to you," Rhodes said.

"I don't have time to talk. I'm in the middle of a big sex scene."

Rhodes looked at her.

"In the book, I mean. I hope you didn't think I had somebody in here with me."

Besides the T-shirt, Vernell was wearing jeans and rubber flip-flops. Her hair was pulled back and held in place with a big plastic clip, and she wasn't wearing any makeup.

"You never know," Rhodes said. "But that's sort of what I wanted to talk to you about."

"Come on in, then," Vernell said. "I'm always willing to talk to a guy about sex. Maybe you could give me some pointers."

"I, um, I —"

134

"For the book, I mean," Vernell said.

Rhodes decided to keep his mouth shut. He didn't like to feel so inarticulate.

They walked back into Vernell's den. Vernell wasn't much of a housekeeper, but it didn't seem to bother her. It didn't bother Rhodes, either.

"Have a seat," Vernell said. She mashed out her cigarette in an ashtray shaped like the state of Texas. "Just shove some of those books out of the way."

Rhodes moved some colorful paperbacks out of a chair. Most of them had pictures of Terry Don Coslin on the cover. Terry Don was a local boy who had made good as a model for romance novel heroes. He had long hair and soulful blue eyes, and he looked great wearing a shirt that appeared not to have any buttons. His abs looked as if they'd been chiseled out of stone. Not that any of those attributes had done him any good when it came right down to it. His death had been the reason for the relative failure of Vernell's writers' conference.

"He was one good-looking man," Vernell said as Rhodes sat down. "Terry Don, I mean."

"I guess so," Rhodes said. "How are your goats?"

Vernell's goats, Shirley, Goodness, and Mercy, were often a cause of concern and controversy in the neighborhood, but Rhodes hadn't heard any complaints about them lately.

"I gave them away," Vernell said. "They

135

needed to be out in the country, and I didn't really have time to fool with them, now that my writing's started to pay off. But you said you came here to talk about sex."

Rhodes didn't remember having put it quite that way. He said, "I came here to talk about Grat Bilson."

"Oh," Vernell said. "Him. I heard he might be dead."

"How'd you hear that?"

"I don't remember. I got a call from someone."

"And you don't remember who?"

"I get a lot of calls. People are always interrupting my work. It could have been anybody."

Rhodes decided to let it go for the moment. He said, "Were you dating Grat Bilson by any chance?"

Vernell looked surprised, then laughed aloud.

"Excuse me for laughing," she said when she'd recovered. "But are you serious?"

"Yes."

"Well, that's just crazy. Grat's married. Why would I date somebody who's married? I might write romance novels, but I'm not trying to live in one."

"Grat's wife thinks you were dating him."

"Yvonne is nutty. You should know that. She runs around with half the men in the county, but she's crazy jealous of her husband. If that's not nutty, I don't know what is. I wouldn't be surprised if she killed Grat."

Rhodes hadn't looked at it quite that way, but he could see how it would fit. Yvonne could have gone out to the deserted house to confront Grat about his supposed infidelity and gotten into an argument with him. If the argument had turned violent, there wasn't much doubt that Yvonne would have hit him with a whiskey bottle. In fact, considering her behavior of earlier that morning, it was even likely that she'd do something like that. If jealousy over Linda Fenton's involvement with Beaman could result in a shooting incident, there was no telling what Yvonne might do if she thought Grat was seeing another woman.

"Of course it's true that I was seeing Grat," Vernell said.

"You were?" Rhodes said.

"Yes, but only on a business basis."

"You might want to explain that."

"He and I were the presidents of the historical associations. You know that those two groups haven't gotten along very well in the past."

Rhodes nodded. He knew only too well.

"Anyway," Vernell said, "Grat and I thought it was time for that to change. We thought it would be for the best if we could work together rather than at cross-purposes. So we'd had a couple of meetings about establishing goals and that sort of thing, trying to see what we could agree on. We even had both groups cooperating pretty well on the Fourth of July celebration. Are you going to be there?"

"I'll be there."

"I don't suppose that Grat will. That's really too bad. He was looking forward to all of it, even the barbecue cook-off."

Rhodes liked the barbecue cook-off. He thought it was the best part of the whole celebration, maybe because it involved eating. Or maybe because, so far as he knew, no one had yet entered any tofu barbecue.

"Did Grat ever happen to mention anything to you about Jay Beaman?" Rhodes asked, getting away from the subject of food.

"Who's Jay Beaman?"

"He's one of the county commissioners."

Vernell said, "I don't follow politics at the local level very much."

Rhodes had long ago stopped being surprised by the number of people who paid no attention to local politics. He thought that was too bad, since the county commissioners controlled quite a chunk of the citizens' tax money. The city didn't control as much, but Rhodes thought people should at least know who was in charge of running things even there. Most people didn't, evidently, and they didn't seem to care much about what happened at the state level, either. Rhodes had seen a newscast not too long before on which a reporter had gone out into the street and asked people if they could name the lieutenant governor of Texas. Of the five people questioned, not a one could come up with the right name.

"Speaking of politics," Vernell went on, "I

suppose I'll have to narrate the historical pageant. If Grat's really dead, I mean."

"You might want to start practicing," Rhodes said. "Just in case."

"I'll do that. But right now I need to work on my sex scene. How about those tips?"

"You're asking the wrong person," Rhodes said.

"I have a feeling you're just being modest."

Rhodes stood up. "Maybe so. But I read one of your books, and I'm not quite up to the standards of the hero."

"Don't let that bother you," Vernell said. "Neither is anybody else."

Rhodes drove back out to the fireworks stand. There was no one around, but someone had come back and closed it, pulling down the canopy in front and back to cover the displays.

The fire trucks were gone from the field, and Rhodes could see their tracks in the burned black grass. He could smell the wet ashes.

He stood there for a few minutes, thinking back over all he knew about the death of Grat Bilson and everything connected to it. There were plenty of suspects, including Yvonne as the current most likely.

Rhodes hadn't entirely dismissed Vernell, either. She was a writer, after all, and writers were liars by profession, as someone had once said. Maybe nothing she'd told him was the truth.

Then there was Linda Fenton, an ex-convict and an arsonist. Who'd put an arsonist in charge of a fireworks stand, anyway? For that matter, who owned the fireworks stands in Blacklin County? Did the same person own them all, or were there multiple owners? It was something that Rhodes had never really thought about before.

Rhodes went to the county car and got Hack on the radio.

"Can you find out who owns the fireworks stands in the county?" he asked.

"That's my job," Hack said. "You ask, I do. You don't have to tell me why. You just tell me what you want, and I find it out."

"Hack," Rhodes said.

"Yes, sir?"

"Are you still pouting?"

"Poutin'? I don't know what you're talkin' about."

"Never mind, then. I appreciate all the hard work you do. And I need that information as soon as you can get it."

"I'll call you," Hack said.

Rhodes signed off and reached into the car to hang the mike on the hook. It was nearly four o'clock in the afternoon, and it was so hot in the car that he'd stood outside to talk.

He thought about who else might want to kill Grat. There was one person who had a sizable motive, and that was Jay Beaman. Rhodes hadn't talked to him yet, and he figured it was about time. He got in the car, started the engine, and turned on the air conditioner. Then he headed for Jay Beaman's precinct office.

18

Rhodes drove past brown fields and by the edge of the county lake. The cracked black mud baked under the lowering sun, and a few droopy cattails grew along the former shoreline. The water had receded so far toward the middle of the lake that Rhodes knew it was just a matter of time before water rationing began for the towns that weren't getting their water from wells. And then the wells would start going dry.

One thing that kept itching at the back of Rhodes's mind was the phone call Jennifer had gotten from Grat Bilson, the call that had informed her of Rhodes's own supposed misuse of county funds. Why had Grat done such a thing? Rhodes didn't have a clue.

Sure, he and Grat had had their problems in the past, but that was all forgotten. Or maybe not. Maybe Grat thought he could settle an old score by getting Rhodes in trouble.

There was a major problem with that theory, however. It was so easy to prove that Rhodes had paid for his house to be painted that the accusation didn't make any sense. Maybe it would later on, Rhodes thought, after he'd found out a few more things.

Jay Beaman's precinct barn looked almost interchangeable with James Allen's. The same kinds of machines were parked under the shed, the long shed, which was painted the same color as the one Allen was in charge of. Rhodes parked the county car and walked to the office, his long shadow going ahead of him across the white gravel.

There was no Mrs. Wilkie working in the office. Beaman's secretary was much younger and blonder. She was chewing gum and working on a crossword puzzle in a book of similar puzzles. The nameplate on her desk informed Rhodes that she was Charlene Fife.

"Is Mr. Beaman in?" Rhodes said.

The woman looked up from the puzzle book and said, "What's a six-letter word for *faithless,* starts with *f?*"

"Fickle," Rhodes said. "F-i-c-k-l-e."

The woman started printing letters in the squares. When she was finished, she said, "That makes sixty-two across *incite.* I should have thought of that." She printed some more letters, then said, "You want to see Mr. Beaman?"

"That's right."

"I'll check to make sure he's here."

She stood up and walked around the desk to knock on the office door.

Maybe the intercom doesn't work, Rhodes thought.

There was a muffled voice from behind the

door, and Charlene opened it for about three inches.

"There's a law officer here to see you," she said.

"Let him in, then. I'm always glad to meet an officer of the law."

"He's in," Charlene said, opening the door wider.

Rhodes walked through. Jay Beaman heaved himself out of his chair and extended his hand across his desk.

They shook hands and Beaman said, "Glad to see you, Sheriff. Charlene, you can shut the door now."

Beaman was a big man, taller than Rhodes and considerably heavier. He looked strong enough to hammer square pegs into round holes using only his fists. He was wearing western-cut slacks, a blue shirt, and a green baseball cap.

Rhodes had never seen Beaman when he wasn't wearing a cap of some kind. In fact, there was a whole group of people these days who always seemed to have caps on. Not high school kids, who usually wore them backward, but adults. They wore them indoors and outdoors. They wore them in stores, and they wore them in restaurants. In offices. For all Rhodes knew, they wore them in church, in the shower, and in bed.

"How's it goin', Sheriff?" Beaman said. "Have a seat and tell me what's on your mind."

Rhodes sat down, but he didn't say what was

on his mind. It wasn't time for that yet. He'd known Beaman for years. Beaman never liked to get right to the point.

So Rhodes sat there while Beaman told him a joke that involved a Texas Aggie, a sheep, and a highway cop. He tried to laugh politely when Beaman got to the punchline, but Beaman laughed loud enough for both of them.

When Beaman was finished laughing, Rhodes nodded toward the computer that sat on its own workstation against the wall.

"You know how to use that thing?" Rhodes asked.

"I know a little bit about it. Not much. Computers are Charlene's department. I just know enough to be dangerous."

"You don't ever surf the Internet?"

"I don't know the Internet from a tennis net," Beaman said, laughing again. "You gonna be at the big barbecue cook-off tomorrow?" he asked when he was through laughing.

"I'll be there," Rhodes said. "How about you?"

Rhodes recalled that Beaman enjoyed the Fourth of July cook-off even more than Rhodes did. In fact, Beaman had won the rib-eating contest for the last three years in a row.

"Wouldn't miss it," Beaman said. "Don't think I'll enter the fun run this year, though."

Rhodes didn't remember that Beaman had entered the fun run any more often than Rhodes had. He said, "Have you talked to a reporter named Jennifer Loam?"

"Whoa, there, Sheriff," Beaman said, putting up his big, rough hands, palms out. "You kinda switched subjects in midstream there."

"I apologize," Rhodes said unapologetically.

Beaman's eyes narrowed. "You better watch how you talk to me, Sheriff. I control the budget for your office."

"You and the other three commissioners," Rhodes said. "But I know you're a fair man. You wouldn't cut my budget just because I was doing my job."

"What's your job got to do with me and that reporter?"

"She thinks you might have been engaged in some criminal activity," Rhodes said.

"That's bull corn. She came around here trying to get me to say something for her story, implying that maybe I'd done something wrong by taking a campaign contribution from a man who got a county contract. Hell, you know all us commissioners would rather deal with somebody we know than with some stranger. So what if the man who gets the contract is a contributor? We know he'll do a fine job."

Rhodes had pretty much known Beaman would say something like that.

"So you wouldn't consider that contribution a bribe."

"No, sir. No way. Ralph Oliver probably gave a contribution to every man on the commissioner's court."

Rhodes didn't doubt it, but that little fact

would make Jennifer Loam's article a lot less interesting. If she ever wrote it.

"What about Linda Fenton?"

Beaman tried not to look at the computer, and he almost managed it.

"Who?" he said.

"Linda Fenton," Rhodes said. "She's supposed to be a friend of yours, or so I've heard."

"Well, you heard wrong. I don't know who that is. Never even heard of her."

It was cool in Beaman's office, but the big man was sweating heavily.

"You're sure?" Rhodes said.

"Sure, I'm sure. Who is she, anyhow?"

"An ex-convict," Rhodes said. "Sent up for arson. It's just as well you don't know her. It might be bad for your political career if people heard you were associating with someone like that. And speaking of arson, I guess you heard about the man who died in a fire the other night."

"I heard. Somebody told me it was Grat Bilson."

"Who told you?"

"I don't remember. Somebody who came by today. Was it Grat who died?"

"Could've been. He hasn't been positively identified yet."

"If it was Grat, that's too bad. Old Grat was a big wheel in the Fourth of July celebration. We'll miss him."

Beaman said it with such sincerity that

Rhodes almost believed him. But then he remembered that Beaman was a politician and had long ago learned how to fake sincerity.

"You have any other questions for me, Sheriff?" Beaman said, and Rhodes knew he was being dismissed. He wasn't ready to leave, however.

"I'd like to know where you were the night Grat, or whoever it was, died in that fire."

"I don't remember," Beaman said.

"It was only a couple of nights ago," Rhodes said.

"I was probably at home. That's where I am, most nights, unless there's a meeting of the court. I don't get out much. A man my age needs his rest."

Beaman had been a year behind Rhodes in school. Rhodes said, "Didn't you used to go to the dog races down in La Marque? I hear those things can go on until pretty late at night, and it's a long drive down there."

"I just go on the weekends, and not but about once a month. Can't stand too much excitement. That all you wanted to know?"

"For now," Rhodes said, standing up. "I'll see you at the cook-off."

"I'll be there," Beaman said, but he looked a little bilious. Rhodes figured the rib-eating title might be up for grabs.

19

Ralph Oliver must have made a lot of money building roads, Rhodes thought. The contractor lived outside the city limits of Clearview in a house that sat on top of a low hill. The house was just a little bit smaller than the county's only country club. It occurred to Rhodes that a man like Oliver had a lot to lose if he were involved in fraud. Oliver had as much of a motive for killing Grat Bilson as anyone if he was guilty of bribing Beaman. And if he knew that there was some kind of investigation being done by a local reporter.

Oliver's lawn covered most of his hill, and it was beautiful. That was the only word for it. And Rhodes could see why. The grass was trimmed perfectly, and it was being watered by a sprinkler system. The water drops sparkled in the late-afternoon sun as they fell. Oliver clearly didn't care that there was a shortage of water in the county. Or he might have had his own private well. Lots of people who lived outside of town had them.

Rhodes drove up the paved semicircular drive to the top of the hill and stopped in front of the house, feeling almost as if he'd driven onto the set of *Gone with the Wind*. There was a fenced pasture in back of the house, and a large metal barn stood on part of it.

Oliver and his wife, Julia, were sitting on the columned porch of the house in white-painted wooden rocking chairs, drinking what appeared to be lemonade. There was a pitcher of it sitting on a white table between their chairs.

"Afternoon, Sheriff," Oliver said when Rhodes got out of the car. "Hot enough for you?"

Rhodes grimaced, and Oliver laughed.

"Just kidding around," he said. "Come on up and have a glass of lemonade with us."

Rhodes said he'd be glad to, and Julia got out of her chair.

"I'll be right back with a glass," she said, and disappeared through the front door.

Oliver stayed in his chair. He was a stocky man with a lot of hair. All over. He was wearing a T-shirt and tennis shorts. Wiry black hairs stuck out of the T-shirt here and there. His legs were hairy all the way up to the shorts, and his head was covered with a tangled mass of thick curls, mostly black but with a little gray mixed in. A tennis racket and a towel lay near his feet.

"Julia and I just finished a game," Oliver said. He picked up the towel and mopped his face, then dropped the towel back on the porch. "The tennis court's out back. I built it so we could get some exercise. Of course with this heat we're having, we're so tired when we finish a set that all we want to do is sit here and watch the traffic on

150

the road. That's what we were doing when we saw you driving along. Sure didn't think you'd be stopping by, though. Is this a social call?"

Rhodes didn't have to answer because Julia came back out. She handed him a glass with a paper napkin wrapped around the bottom.

"Let me pour for you, Sheriff," Julia said.

She was about forty, with short blond hair and an athletic build. She looked a lot more like a tennis player than her husband did.

When she'd finished pouring, she handed Rhodes the glass and sat down. There was an extra chair, so Rhodes sat in it and sipped his lemonade. It was sweet and cold, and it felt good going down his throat, which was still scratchy from all the smoke he'd inhaled.

"You asked whether this was a social call," Rhodes said when he'd drunk about half the lemonade. "It isn't. Not exactly. I came by to ask you if you knew a man named Grat Bilson."

"Grat?" Oliver said. "Sure, I know Grat. Everybody knows Grat, isn't that right Julia?" Julia nodded, and Oliver went on. "He's a big wheel in the historical society. What about him?"

"Somebody killed him," Rhodes said, even though he still wasn't positive. He just wanted to get Oliver's reaction.

Oliver looked down at his tennis shoes and sipped at his lemonade. After a couple of seconds, he said, "Damn shame. Grat was an okay guy. What's his dying got to do with me, though?"

"Probably nothing," Rhodes said. "Seen Jay Beaman lately?"

"Good old Jay. Haven't seen him in a week or two. Don't tell me he's dead, too."

"No, he's not dead. At least I don't think he is. He was fine when I talked to him about half an hour ago."

"Good. I'd hate to think there was a serial killer going around the county. Did you get the fella that killed Grat?"

"Not yet," Rhodes said. "But I'm working on it."

"How'd he die?"

"Somebody hit him in the head, then burned him up."

Oliver mopped his face with the towel again. He tossed it down and said, "Jesus. That's terrible."

Julia didn't say anything, but she nodded in agreement.

"I have one more question for you," Rhodes said. "Do you know a woman named Linda Fenton?"

Oliver cut his eyes toward his wife, who didn't seem to notice. She was sipping lemonade and looking down across the lawn at the road.

"I don't think I ever heard of her," Oliver said. "Does she live around here?"

"That's what *I'd* like to know," Rhodes said.

Rhodes went by the jail after his talk with Oliver. He hadn't learned much more from either

Oliver or Beaman than he'd known to begin with, but he did discover that they were both liars. In fact, he was pretty sure that they were both lying about the same person, Linda Fenton, not that Rhodes blamed them. He'd probably lie too if he were involved with an ex-convict who'd been guilty of arson, especially if a man had just died in a suspicious house fire.

"Any calls?" Rhodes asked when he walked into the jail.

"Dr. Lewis," Hack said. "He says that there's no doubt about who died in that fire."

"Grat Bilson," Rhodes said.

"Right," Lawton said, walking in from the cell block.

"I'm the one who's supposed to tell him that," Hack said. "It was me Dr. Lewis called, not you."

"Sorry about that," Lawton said, not looking sorry at all.

"What about Ruth?" Rhodes asked before the two old men could get started on each other. "Has she had any luck finding Linda Fenton?"

"Nope," Hack said. "Or if she has, she hasn't called in. You sent Ruth chasing after that Fenton woman, but you didn't give her much to go on."

What he meant, of course, was that he wanted Rhodes to tell him all about Linda Fenton. But Rhodes wasn't going to do that just yet.

"I didn't have much," Rhodes said, wishing he'd thought to look at the license number of

153

the old pickup that had been parked by the fire-works stand. He wondered if Jennifer Loam had. He'd have to call and ask.

But first he wanted to know what Hack had found out about the fireworks stands.

"You'd be surprised how hard it is to find out stuff like that," Hack said. "Especially when somebody doesn't want you to know."

"You couldn't just look in the court records? The tax rolls?"

"It's not all that easy," Lawton said. "Some-times —"

"Who's the one who did all the work?" Hack asked.

"You are," Lawton said, "but —"

"But, nothin'. I'm the one who did the work, so I'm the one who tells the story."

"Fine," Lawton said. "Glory hog."

"I'm not hoggin' anything. I just said that I'm the one who did the work, so I'm the one —"

"Never mind," Rhodes said. "Just get to the point."

"That's what I was tryin' to do," Hack said. "But Lawton wouldn't let me. He kept buttin' in." Hack stopped and smiled. "Buttin' in. Get it? He kept saying *but,* so he was buttin' in."

"I get it," Rhodes said. "Now finish what you were telling me."

Hack drummed his fingers on the desk as if trying to gather his thoughts. He said, "Like I was sayin', it's not always easy to find out who owns things. Sometimes the owner is just a name, like a corporation. The Big Bang Corporation, for example."

"So what you have to do," Lawton said, "is find the owner of the corporation."

"I'm not gonna tell this if he keeps buttin' in," Hack said, not smiling this time.

Rhodes looked at Lawton, who shrugged his shoulders.

"Go on," Rhodes told Hack.

"Sometimes you can't even find the owner of the corporation," Hack said. "I guess you could if you knew more about computers than I do, or if you had a month or so to dig around in the courthouse."

"So what you're telling me is that you didn't find out who owned the fireworks stands."

"No, I'm not tellin' you that."

"It sure sounds like it."

"That's because you keep interruptin' me."

"I beg your pardon," Rhodes said.

"That's okay," Hack said. "I'm used to it. There's something else I'm used to, too. You want me to tell you things, but you don't ever tell me what's goin' on around here."

Rhodes knew that Hack still wanted to know about Linda Fenton, but he wasn't ready to get into that.

"You first," Rhodes said. "Then me."

"That's right. You're the sheriff, and I'm just —"

"Never mind that. Tell me about the fireworks stands."

"All right. If you want to be that way about it, I'll tell you. What it boils down to is that I was able to get somebody in the courthouse, somebody who has a better computer than I do, to do a search of all kinds of documents on a state level. She could get access to some stuff that I didn't even know about, so she found out who owns most of the fireworks stands in this county."

"And that would be?"

"The Big Bang Corporation."

"You've already told me that."

"Yeah," Lawton said. "But he didn't tell you who the corporation president was. He told me, though. Want me to tell you?"

"If you do," Hack said, "I'll never tell you anything again."

"You never tell me anything anyway, about half the time. I bet you tell Miz McGee, though. I bet you tell her all kinds of things."

Hack pushed his chair away from the desk and started to get up.

"That's enough," Rhodes said. "Both of you simmer down. I need to know who owns those fireworks stands, and I need to know right now. So who is it?"

"It's Jay Beaman," Hack said.

Well, thought Rhodes, *that explains how Linda Fenton got her job.*

20

James Allen, like Ralph Oliver, lived outside the city limits. Before Allen had become a commissioner, he'd been a bulldozer operator. He and his wife lived in a small house, and as they had more and more children, the house had gotten bigger and bigger. Instead of building a new home, they'd simply added more rooms onto the one they already owned. It was an interesting bit of architecture, and it was in remarkably good repair. There was a paved road leading up to it, and the whole place practically gleamed in the dusky twilight. The yard, while not quite up to the standards set by Ralph Oliver, was still quite green. There was no sprinkler system that Rhodes could see, however.

Allen came out of the front door almost as soon as Rhodes stepped out of the county car.

"I hope I'm not interrupting your supper," Rhodes said.

"Not at all," Allen said. "Margie's still working on it. Some of the kids are helping. What are you doing out here in the country?"

"I just found out something I thought you might be interested in knowing," Rhodes said.

"What's that?"

"I was doing a little snooping, and I found out who owns all the fireworks stands in the county."

"Probably some yankee," Allen said, smiling.

For some people in Blacklin County, a yankee was anyone who lived north of Dallas.

"It's Jay Beaman," Rhodes said.

For a full ten seconds, Allen didn't say anything. He just stood there, looking at Rhodes. Finally he said, "You must be kidding."

"I'm not kidding."

"You mean to tell me that after all the time I've spent on trying to get fireworks under control, Jay Beaman's been selling them?"

"That's right. No wonder you never got any support from him."

"I never got much support from anybody. I wouldn't be surprised if the other commissioners were in on this with him."

"They're not," Rhodes said. "Or at least they don't own any stands. It's all Beaman."

"Then he must lobby them on the sly. I've never gotten anywhere with any of them."

"It could be that they just like fireworks," Rhodes said.

"There's nothing wrong with fireworks," Allen said. "Except that they can be dangerous and start fires. I hear you found out about that this afternoon."

Rhodes grinned ruefully. "I found out, all right. The hard way."

"I appreciate it that you let me know about

this," Allen said. "I'll talk to Beaman and try to get him to listen to reason."

"Do you think anybody else might have known he owned those stands?"

"Not unless it was the other commissioners. I don't see how he managed to keep it a secret, though."

Rhodes didn't know, either. He wondered if Grat Bilson had found out. If he had, it might have given Linda Fenton and Beaman another reason to kill him.

"It was a secret from me," Rhodes said.

"Me, too," Allen told him.

"Maybe I can use it," Rhodes said.

"What for?"

"I think maybe Beaman can tell me something about Grat Bilson's death."

"You don't think he had anything to do with it, do you?"

"You never can tell, but even if he didn't, I think he knows things that he's keeping secret. The fireworks stands are just part of it."

"Grat and Jay never liked each other. I wouldn't be surprised to hear that Jay killed him. Jay doesn't like people who get in his way."

"Who does?" Rhodes said.

"I guess most of us don't. Jay gets more upset than most, though. I've seen him throw some real fits."

"He seems calm enough at the court meetings."

"Maybe so, but you've never seen him in private. I wouldn't put it past him to kill someone. And then there's Yvonne. She was the one who started the fire today, shooting off a pistol, right?"

"That's right," Rhodes said.

"I wouldn't put it past Yvonne to have killed Grat. They had all kinds of trouble. It had to be either Yvonne or Jay, don't you think?"

"That's what I'm trying to find out," Rhodes said.

Rhodes got Hack on the radio and asked how Yvonne Bilson was doing.

"She's not happy," Hack said. "But she's not causin' any trouble. Lawton says she's just curled up in her cell and not sayin' much."

"He might want to check on her now and then. If Ruth comes in, have her take a look, too. We don't want anything to happen to her."

"Nothin's gonna happen. She's not suicidal, just depressed."

Rhodes thought Hack was right, and he wondered what was depressing Yvonne more, Grat's death or the fact that she was in jail.

"I want you to do something for me," Rhodes told Hack.

"What's that?"

Rhodes told him to call Jennifer Loam.

"She might still be at the newspaper office, or she might have gone home," Rhodes said. "Find her and ask if she got the license number of the pickup that was parked at the fireworks stand this afternoon."

"Don't need to," Hack said. "She called right after you left. Said she was sorry she hadn't called sooner but that she forgot in all the excitement. Said she thought maybe you'd gotten the number, what with you bein' a professional lawman and all."

"I was busy," Rhodes said, but he knew he should have been more alert. "Did you get the number to Ruth?"

"Yep. Did somethin' else, too."

"What?"

"Checked with the DMV to see who owned the truck. Want to guess?"

"Why don't you just tell me."

"I bet you could figure it out if you just gave it a second or two."

"Jay Beaman," Rhodes said.

"See? I knew you could do it. That's why you're the sheriff, and I'm just —"

"All right," Rhodes said. "If Ruth catches up with that truck, you let me know."

"That's my job," Hack said. "You can count on me. Even if you don't —"

Rhodes signed off before he could finish.

When Rhodes got out of the county car at his house, he could hear Yancey yipping and yapping at the back door. Speedo walked over to Rhodes and looked up at him.

"You think he makes too much noise?" Rhodes said.

Aside from wagging his tail, Speedo didn't answer, not that Rhodes had really expected him to.

"Well, I think he does," Rhodes said. He bent down and rubbed Speedo's head. "I guess we'd better let him out. Maybe he'll calm down."

Speedo looked doubtful, and Rhodes didn't blame him. Rhodes walked over to the back door. Speedo, after a moment's hesitation, followed along. When Rhodes opened the door, Yancey tumbled out like a cotton ball on legs, still yipping, and immediately started chasing Speedo all over the yard.

Rhodes wondered if Speedo was running because the smaller dog was so annoying or if Speedo just liked playing chase. Not that it mattered, but Rhodes thought that it was the latter. In fact, both dogs seemed to be having a wonderful time in spite of the fact that it was still over ninety degrees. So Rhodes left them to it and went inside.

Ivy looked up from the book she was reading when Rhodes came into the den.

"What happened to you?" she asked.

"When?" Rhodes said.

"All day. I heard that you had a fistfight with a woman and then mud-wrestled with her."

"You've been talking to Hack again, haven't you."

"Maybe," Ivy said. "Or maybe I just looked in the clothes hamper."

162

Rhodes had finally told Hack all about Linda Fenton and janesinjail.com, so he was the logical source of Ivy's information. The singed and muddy clothes would merely have confirmed what Hack told Ivy.

"What about the bathroom?" he asked.

"The tub was awfully clean," Ivy said. "Cleaner than it's been in a day or two, at least. I assume that someone must have messed it up pretty badly and then tried to cover his tracks."

"You should have been a cop," Rhodes said.

"I thought it would be easier just to marry one. Now tell me all about it."

"How much do you know?" Rhodes asked.

Ivy closed the book after putting a piece of paper in it to mark her place.

"Not as much as I'd like to," she said.

"Why don't we go out for something to eat, and I'll give you the whole seamy story," Rhodes said.

"Good idea," Ivy said. "Where shall we eat?"

"I could use a hamburger."

"Not from McDonald's, I'll bet."

"I was thinking the Bluebonnet."

"Sounds good to me," Ivy said.

The Bluebonnet was at the edge of town, out past the Wal-Mart. It had been there for as long as Rhodes could remember, and it had served the same kind of hamburgers for just as long. The meat was cooked on a grill that you could see from where you were sitting. You could smell the meat frying, and you could listen to the pop and sizzle of the fat while you waited. The tables were wobbly, and the old wooden floor wasn't level, not even close, but that didn't bother Rhodes. He wasn't there to check the store's foundation.

"Want some French fries to go with your burger?" he asked Ivy.

"How about onion rings, too?" Ivy said.

"That's pretty scary," Rhodes said.

"What is?"

"You can read my mind."

"As if that were a tough trick," Ivy said.

Rhodes ordered the burgers, fries, and onion rings. Then he got a couple of Dr Peppers out of the cooler. They were in twenty-ounce plastic bottles, but that was better than cans.

"You know what David Letterman said about Dr Pepper, don't you," Ivy said when Rhodes put the bottles on the table.

"No, and I'm not sure I want to."

"You probably don't. Let's just say it wasn't very nice. But what does he know?"

"Nothing about soft drinks," Rhodes said, taking a big swallow.

"You're right," Ivy said. "Now while we're waiting for our hamburgers, why don't you tell me about what happened this afternoon."

"You want the long version or the short version?"

"Whichever one is the best."

"The long one has those seamy details I

mentioned," Rhodes said. "We'll start with janesinjail.com and go on from there."

"Janes in jail? That sounds like the name of a bad made-for-cable movie."

"It gets worse."

"Oh, good," Ivy said. "That's what I've been waiting to hear. It sounds like a good story."

"It is," Rhodes said.

"So tell me."

Rhodes did.

21

By the time Rhodes finished telling Ivy about his day, the hamburgers and fries were gone. There was one onion ring left, and Rhodes was eyeing it. He thought that Ivy had eaten more of the rings than he had, so he clearly deserved the last one.

Ivy read his mind again.

"Go ahead," she said. "You can have it."

Rhodes didn't wait to hear more. He picked up the onion ring and bit off half of it.

While he was enjoying it, Ivy said, "I think Vernell did it."

Rhodes ate the other half of the onion ring before he spoke. Then he said, "Why Vernell?"

"Because it seems like every time there's a murder, she's right in the middle of it."

"That's not her fault. More like a case of being in the wrong place at the wrong time, or maybe associating with the wrong people. Or even just plain bad luck. What do you want for dessert?"

"Reese's peanut butter cups."

"Excellent choice," Rhodes said.

He went to the candy counter and picked up two packages of Reese's. Then he paid for them and went back to the table. He handed Ivy her candy and opened his own.

"You realize that we've consumed about a three months' quota of fat grams tonight, I guess," Ivy said.

Rhodes knew she was right. His hands and face were still greasy from the meal. But he didn't care. He ate one of the Reese's and smiled.

Ivy said, "So you don't think Vernell did it?"

"I'm not sure," Rhodes said. "I wouldn't rule her out, but so far I can't come up with a motive for her. Even if she was dating Grat, like Yvonne said, there's no reason for her to kill him."

Ivy licked chocolate off her fingers. She said, "Maybe Vernell wants to be president of both historical societies."

"I don't think she'd kill somebody for that reason."

"She'd have to be crazy," Ivy admitted. "What about Yvonne as the killer?"

"She had a motive, all right," Rhodes said. "But if she killed Grat, why go after Linda Fenton?"

"To make herself look innocent. If you believed she blamed the Fenton woman, you wouldn't blame her."

"You think Yvonne's that devious?"

"Don't you?"

Rhodes wasn't sure. Yvonne had seemed genuinely grief-stricken when he'd first talked to her, but even at the time he hadn't been sure how much of the grief was real and how much was show. The attack on Linda Fenton could have been just another act, if Ivy was right.

"What about Linda Fenton?" Ivy said, breaking in on his thoughts. "Tell me a little more about that janesinjail.com."

"You know as much as I do," Rhodes said. Then he had an idea. "Why don't we go by the jail and have Hack check it out? It might be interesting."

"I'm sure it would," Ivy said.

Hack had already checked it out.

"I thought we might be able to get Lawton a date," he said. "One of those prison women might take him even if nobody else would. They're bound to be desperate."

"Plenty of women around here'd go out with me if I asked 'em," Lawton said. "And not just desperate ones, either. I just don't think it's seemly for old geezers like me and you to be chasin' after women."

"What's that supposed to mean?" Hack said.

Lawton started to answer, but Rhodes didn't give him the chance. He said, "It means that we came here to look at the computer, not listen to you two. Come on, Hack, let's see what you can find."

Hack glared at Lawton, but he turned to the computer and typed in the URL. In a few seconds the screen for janesinjail was displayed.

"See?" Hack said. "I think that razor-wire background is a nice touch."

Ivy leaned forward and peered at the screen.

"Something for everyone," she said. "You can pick your preferred age range and ethnic group. And look down there." She tapped a fingernail on the screen. "There's even a bisexual and lesbian category."

Hack blushed. "Me and Lawton didn't look at any of the pictures. I didn't go past this first page."

"Well," Rhodes said, "let's have a look at the pictures."

They'd decided on the age group when the radio crackled. It was Ruth Grady, and she'd found Linda Fenton. Or if not Linda Fenton, the truck from the fireworks stand. It was at Jay Beaman's house.

"You should've thought of lookin' for it there, yourself," Hack told Rhodes.

"I know. Ask her what she's done."

Ruth hadn't done anything. She'd located the truck and then called in to let Rhodes know.

"Tell her I'll be right there," Rhodes said. "Ivy, you want to go for a ride-along?"

"Can we use the siren?"

"I don't think so. I wouldn't want anyone to know we're coming."

"That's too bad, but I'll go anyway. I've always wanted to be in on a bust."

"I'm not going to bust anybody. I'm just going to do some talking."

169

"Sounds pretty dull. I thought your life was filled with adventure and excitement."

"Only when I'm mud-wrestling," Rhodes said.

Beaman lived in Thurston, in a two-storied house that had been built in the early part of the century and looked it. The place needed paint, and the yard looked even worse than Rhodes's. A few scraggly weeds poked through the dirt, but grass was almost nonexistent. The house was dark except for the first floor, where there was a light shining through the curtains in one of the rooms.

Ruth Grady was parked about a block away. The county car was pulled into an old service station. The gas pumps had been removed because the place had been closed for years. In fact, most of the businesses in Thurston had been closed for a good while. Rhodes was afraid that before too many more years had passed, Thurston would go the way of Milsby.

He stopped the county car next to Ruth's and got out.

"Seen anything?" he asked.

"Not much. I didn't get here until Beaman was already home. The pickup's parked around back. It was already here, too. I haven't seen anybody moving around in there, but that's because the curtains are closed."

"And nobody's left?"

"I'm not sure. I had to decide whether to watch the front or the back, so here I am. Nobody's left through the front door, but that's all I know. What do we do now?"

"I'm going to pay a visit," Rhodes said. "You and Ivy can wait here." He started to get back in the car, then thought better of it. "Maybe you'd better not wait here. Ivy can stay in my car. You pull around the block and watch the back in case anyone tries to leave that way."

Ruth nodded, started the car, and drove away. Rhodes got back into his own car.

"What's the plan?" Ivy asked when Rhodes returned.

"I'm going to knock on the door and see who answers it," Rhodes said.

"Sounds simple enough."

"My plans always sound simple," Rhodes said. "But for some reason they don't always work out."

"Robert Burns had something to say about that."

"I had to memorize that poem in high school. I wonder if kids still memorize stuff."

"Rap music," Ivy said.

"I think I prefer Burns."

"Which just shows how old you are."

"Thanks for reminding me," Rhodes said.

Beaman had changed into jeans, a cotton shirt, and walking shoes. He was, however, still wearing the baseball cap. He had a can of beer in one hand.

"Sheriff," he said when he opened the door.

171

"Two visits in one day. I must be doing something right. Or wrong. Which is it?"

"That's what I'm here to find out," Rhodes told him. "Can I come in?"

"Sure, sure. Want a beer?"

"No thanks. Do you have company?"

"Company?"

"Is there anyone else here?"

"No, nobody at all. My wife died five years ago, and I've lived by myself ever since. Come on in. You'll have to excuse the mess, though. I'm not much of a housekeeper."

Rhodes went inside. Beaman hadn't been exaggerating about the mess. A dirty shirt hung on the back of a chair, and an empty beer can sat on the coffee table, along with a half-empty glass of water. Or maybe the glass was half full. Rhodes was never sure about that. There was also a heavy glass ashtray, but there were no ashes in it. Beaman didn't smoke, so maybe the ashtray was left over from his marriage. The hardwood floor was a little gritty underfoot, and Rhodes guessed it hadn't been swept or mopped since George Bush (the younger) had assumed the presidency.

There was some dried mud on the couch. Rhodes reached over and picked up a piece of it.

"Told you I wasn't much of a housekeeper," Beaman said.

Rhodes wished he'd brought an evidence bag in with him, but he hadn't thought about it. He dropped the mud in his shirt pocket and said, "I think there's someone else here."

"Nope," Beaman said. "Just me, myself, and I."

"You're sure about that?"

"Sure as I can be."

"Then you won't mind if I look around?"

"Help yourself," Beaman said, gesturing with his arm. "I have nothing to hide."

Rhodes was about to take him up on the offer when he heard a horn honking outside. He and Beaman went to the door and looked out. Ivy was standing beside the county car, motioning for Rhodes to come out and join her.

He excused himself to Beaman and went to the car.

"What's the trouble?" he asked.

"Ruth called me on the radio," Ivy said. "She said to tell you that the pickup's not parked in the back anymore."

No wonder Beaman was feeling so expansive, Rhodes thought. He went back to the house and told Beaman that he'd be leaving.

"Got to rush off to catch some crooks?" Beaman said.

"No," Rhodes told him. "I'm going to look for a stolen truck."

"I hope you find it," Beaman said.

"Me too," Rhodes told him.

"Who does it belong to, anyway?"

"You," Rhodes said.

22

Ruth was upset, but Rhodes told her not to worry about it. It wasn't her fault that Linda Fenton had hit the road.

"They must have seen me," Ruth said. "I tried to find a better place to park, but there's not one."

She was right about that, Rhodes thought. In Thurston the streets were virtually deserted twenty-four hours a day, except for a few cars in front of Hod Barrett's grocery. But that was only during the daylight hours.

"I should have parked around back," Ruth said. "That way, she couldn't have slipped by me."

"She might just have come out the front," Rhodes said. "We'll find her tomorrow. Or maybe tonight."

He called Hack on the radio and told him to get out an APB on the pickup.

"Did that already," Hack said. "Just in case. Not that I ever get any credit for thinkin' on the job."

"Is it just me?" Rhodes asked Ivy when he'd signed off, "or is Hack getting more crotchety these days?"

"It's just you," Ivy said.

"I was afraid you'd say that."

"What are you going to do now that your suspect has flown the coop?"

"Go home and go to bed."

"Sounds like a good idea. You have a tough day coming up tomorrow. It's the Fourth of July, and you have an ongoing murder case. You need your rest."

As usual, things didn't work out exactly as Rhodes had planned. When he got home, the telephone was ringing. He answered, and Jennifer Loam said, "I need to talk to you. It's important."

"Come on over," Rhodes said. "Do you know where I live?"

Jennifer said she didn't know, and Rhodes gave her directions.

"Is that a dog I hear?" Jennifer said.

"By some definitions, I guess," Rhodes said. "Are you afraid of dogs?"

"No. I like dogs. Is yours friendly?"

Rhodes looked down at Yancey, who was bouncing up and down in excitement.

"You might say that."

"Good. I'll be there in a few minutes."

Rhodes hung up and told Ivy what the call had been about and said that Jennifer Loam would be coming over.

"I wonder if she drinks coffee," Ivy said.

"I think all reporters drink coffee. It's one of the job requirements."

"It's a job requirement for cops, too, and you don't drink it."

"That's because I'm odd."

Ivy smiled. "You can say that again."

Jennifer Loam sat across from Rhodes at his kitchen table while Yancey sniffed around her feet, pausing to yap furiously now and then. Ivy poured coffee for herself and Jennifer, then gave Rhodes a glass of water.

"Here's the problem," Jennifer told Rhodes. "I can't prove anything for my story. I told you the other afternoon that I was still investigating, but so far I haven't found a thing that really shows Jay Beaman took a bribe from Ralph Oliver. He got a big contribution, but so did some of the other commissioners."

"So all that information you were developing turns out to be more or less worthless."

Jennifer gently shoved Yancey away from her feet, but Yancey came right back. He was nothing if not persistent.

"I guess you could put it that way," Jennifer said. "Since I found out that what I was told about you was a lie, I'm wondering if any of what Mr. Bilson said was true. Except for the part about the ex-convict Beaman was dating. That was her at the fireworks stand, wasn't it?"

"Yes," Rhodes said, "and it was quick thinking on your part to get the license number of the truck she was driving. It belongs to Jay Beaman, by the way."

Rhodes didn't mind letting Jennifer know about the truck, but he wasn't going to tell her about Beaman's being the owner of the fireworks stand, not just yet. She'd have to develop that information on her own, or wait until Rhodes was ready to reveal it.

"Did you find the truck?" Jennifer asked.

"It was at Jay's house, but it's gone now. I don't know where."

"This hasn't worked out at all," Jennifer said. "I thought I had a big story, and all I wind up with is nothing. Unless you can add something to what I've found out."

Rhodes realized that the reason for Jennifer's visit was not just to tell him that she'd come up with no solid data for her story but to pump him for information. He had some, of course, but he wasn't going to give it out just yet. He didn't want Beaman to find out that anyone knew about the fireworks stands.

"There's been a murder," Rhodes said. "You could report that."

Jennifer drank some of her coffee and said, "That's very good. Is it flavored?"

"Hazelnut," Ivy said.

"I thought so." She took another sip. "Anyway, I did report the murder, Sheriff. Didn't you read today's paper?"

"Haven't had the chance," Rhodes said.

"I did," Ivy said. "It was a very good story."

"Thanks."

"And I can give you a follow-up," Rhodes told

177

Jennifer. "The body's been positively identified. It was Grat Bilson, all right."

"I know that. I called the jail late this afternoon, and Mr. Wilson told me. I've already done a story for tomorrow's paper. It would be a better story, though, if you'd solved the murder."

"I'm working on that," Rhodes said.

"Do you think Mr. Beaman did it?"

Rhodes thought that Jennifer sounded unduly hopeful. If Beaman was the killer, maybe he'd confess to taking bribes while in office.

"I hope Beaman didn't kill anybody," Rhodes said. "It wouldn't look good if one of our commissioners was a killer."

"He could've done it to cover up his bribe-taking."

"Campaign contributions," Rhodes said.

"Whatever. I'm sure Mr. Bilson would've gotten me some solid information if he'd only lived long enough."

"Pretty inconsiderate of him to go and get murdered," Rhodes said.

Jennifer's coffee cup clinked as she set it in the saucer.

"I sounded selfish, didn't I?" she said. "Here I am worrying about my story, and poor Mr. Bilson's dead."

"He's not worried about anything," Rhodes said, "not even who killed him."

"It was his wife, I suppose," Jennifer said. "She acted pretty crazy this afternoon."

"I wouldn't make up my mind about who's

178

guilty just yet," Rhodes told her. "It might turn out to be Beaman after all."

Jennifer didn't say she hoped so, but Rhodes could tell she was thinking it.

"Will you be at the Fourth of July celebration tomorrow?" she asked.

"I'll be there."

"What about the commissioners?"

"They'll be there, too. Some of them, anyway."

"Good. I think I'll try talking to Mr. Beaman again."

"He usually enters the rib-eating contest," Rhodes said.

"What about you?"

"I thought about it," Rhodes said. "But I'm more the fun-run type."

Ivy was still laughing about that when they went to bed.

23

It was so hot when Rhodes walked out of the house the next morning that he was sure the Fourth of July would be the hottest day of the year so far. That meant the temperature would be over a hundred degrees. It wouldn't have to go far to get there. Rhodes doubted that it had gotten below ninety all night, and there was a slight breeze that felt as if it might be blowing out of an overheated oven. Rhodes hoped the fun runners didn't all get heat stroke.

He fed and watered Speedo, who didn't appear eager to do any romping around the yard. Rhodes thought that showed the dog's intelligence.

Ivy came to the door just before Rhodes got in the county car and told him that she'd see him later at the park.

"I don't want to stay the whole day," she said. "I'm afraid I'll dry up and blow away."

"You're going to miss the fun run," Rhodes said.

Ivy laughed. "Right. So are you. And here I thought you were going to compete this year."

"Maybe next year," Rhodes said. "I'll see you at the park."

The park wasn't as crowded as Rhodes had thought it might be. He was able to find a shady parking spot under an elm tree, which meant he might actually be able to get back into his car without suffering second-degree burns from contact with the seat covers.

The first runners were crossing the finish line for the fun run when Rhodes walked up. Sweat was streaming off them, and they all looked ready for a cold shower. And all they'd have to show for it was a T-shirt, though the top finishers in each age group would get a cheap plastic trophy. Rhodes shook his head in wonder.

He looked at the bandstand, which was draped with red, white, and blue streamers. There was no band on it yet, just as there was no one on the softball field. Later in the afternoon the historical pageant would be held there, with, Rhodes supposed, Vernell Lindsey as the narrator.

The barbecue cooks were already hard at work. Rhodes could smell the aromatic smoke from the various kinds of wood that they were burning in their cookers. Some used mesquite, some used oak, and others wouldn't tell what kind of wood they used. The secrecy was an important part of the mystique. The smoke would have smelled better to him, he supposed, if he hadn't inhaled so much of it the previous day.

When the wood was burned down to coals,

the actual cooking would begin, with the meat being basted by all kinds of secret barbecue sauces, the recipes having been handed down from fathers to their children for generations. People in Texas took their barbecue seriously. As far as most of them were concerned, barbecue couldn't really be called barbecue if it was cooked in any other state.

While Rhodes watched, a yellow-and-black school bus pulled up near the bandstand. When it stopped, the door opened and students filed out. A truck loaded with instruments drove up beside the bus, and a pickup with a bed full of folding chairs wasn't far behind.

Before long, the folding chairs were set up on the bandstand, the players were sitting in them, and the strains of Sousa marches drifted out over the park. Rhodes had always liked marches, not that he was very good at marching. He just liked the sound of the music. He could identify "Stars and Stripes Forever," "King Cotton," and a few others. He had a feeling he'd be hearing them a lot that day.

Someone from the local radio station, KCLR, or K-Clear as the announcers liked to call it, was working around a sound truck, getting set up for live broadcasting. Rhodes figured that the listeners would get tired of marches before the day was over and might tune out before the historical pageant.

There were flea market booths set up all along the street that ran through the park, and Rhodes thought he ought to check out a few of them just to see what was there.

He was in the fourth or fifth one, looking over a stack of rusty tools that the owner was offering to sell Rhodes for what he said was a fraction of their real value, when James Allen came up and asked if Rhodes would like a Dr Pepper.

"Anytime," Rhodes said, leaving the tools behind without regret.

He followed Allen to a tent where the band parents were selling soft drinks. In cans. But Rhodes supposed a canned drink was better than nothing, and Allen was buying, so he couldn't complain.

"Help yourself," the man behind the counter said when Allen paid him.

"What'll you have?" Rhodes asked Allen, who said he'd take a Pepsi.

The cans were kept in a tub of ice, so Rhodes plunged his hand in, shoving ice around and looking for a Dr Pepper and a Pepsi. After a few seconds, his hand was nearly frozen, but he located the cans and pulled them out.

Allen took the Pepsi and brushed off a couple of small pieces of ice that were still clinging to the can. Then he handed Rhodes a paper towel to wrap the Dr Pepper in. The towel soaked up the cold water on the can, and Rhodes could hold it without losing all the feeling in his fingers.

He and Allen walked out under the elm trees and stood in the shade, drinking their drinks, listening to the band, and smelling the smoke from the barbecue cookers.

The cookers were nearly all homemade from black sheet metal, and there were large cookers and small ones, mostly large, most of them so large, in fact, that they were hauled in trailers. Some, even larger, were on wheels, and they were the trailers.

Rhodes saw Jennifer Loam interviewing one of the women who was carefully basting a brisket with some of her specially made sauce. Rhodes figured Jennifer's heart wasn't really in it. Covering a barbecue cook-off wasn't nearly as exciting as breaking a big story about corruption in county government.

Another truck drove into the park while Rhodes and Allen were watching. The cooker behind it was trailing sparks like the tail of a comet. Rhodes thought of the fireworks stand.

"Must've started the fire early," Allen said, "so it'd be cooked down to coals by the time it got here."

"I don't like the looks of those sparks," Rhodes said, and almost as soon as the words were out of his mouth, they heard the fire sirens.

Rhodes tossed his empty can in a recycling bin and headed for his car. When he drove out of the park, he looked into his rearview mirror.

Jennifer Loam was right behind him.

At first Rhodes was afraid the whole town might be burning, but it turned out that only the grass in some ditches near some vacant lots had caught fire. There was no way to say for sure that the cooker Rhodes and Allen had seen was the cause of the fire, but Rhodes figured there wasn't much doubt. If it didn't rain soon, they'd have to consider banning barbecue cookers unless people could use a little common sense.

Chief Parker's men were able to get the fire put out before it did much damage, though it did scorch a couple of big trees near the ditches.

Rhodes managed to have a few words with Parker during a lull in the fire-fighting, and Parker told him that the preliminary report indicated that the accelerants used at Grat Bilson's place had indeed been alcohol and gasoline.

"Did you send that bottle off for fingerprinting?" Parker asked Rhodes.

Rhodes looked around for Jennifer Loam, who was too far away to hear. She was writing in her notebook and not even looking in Rhodes's direction.

"We did the printing," Rhodes told Parker. "We don't have a report yet on whether there are any matches in the files for the prints we got. We sent the bottle off for testing to see if there were any traces of hair or blood on it. We didn't see any, but that doesn't mean there weren't some there."

"I'm sure Grat's are on there."

"There were two sets. Maybe we'll find out who the others belong to. Or maybe we won't."

"Good luck," Parker said.

Rhodes admitted that he'd need it.

When Rhodes returned to the park, James Allen was still standing in the shade of some elm trees not too far from where Rhodes parked. But this time Rhodes had to park in the sun. All the shady spots were taken.

"You don't look any the worse for wear," Allen said when Rhodes got out of the county car.

"The fire department didn't need any help," Rhodes said. "What's been going on here?"

"Not much. That fire reminds me, how's your investigation going?"

"I don't know," Rhodes said. "I have plenty of suspects and plenty of motives, but no good answers."

"What do you think about Beaman?"

"Beaman?"

"He and Grat never did get along. Grat was snooping around more than he had any right to, and Jay didn't like that. He was afraid Grat would find out too much."

"What was there to find out?" Rhodes asked.

"You know. What we were talking about the other day."

"I don't think the reporter has any proof of that."

He looked around the park for Jennifer, but he didn't see her anywhere. She was probably at the newspaper office, working on a story about the fire.

"The only reason there's no proof is because Grat's dead," Allen said. "I think I'll go see if the barbecue's ready. See you later."

He walked away, and Rhodes saw that one of the barbecue cookers was Ralph Oliver. Oliver was wearing a chef's hat and a white apron. His wife was with him, but she wasn't wearing a hat or apron. Oliver waved a sauce brush at Rhodes, who waved back.

Allen went over and started talking to Oliver, while Rhodes went to look for Ivy. He hoped she'd make it in time for the rib-eating contest. He thought he might enter this year.

Ivy arrived in plenty of time, and Rhodes told her his plan.

"You'll do better in that contest than you would have in the fun run," Ivy said.

There was a long table set up on the shady side of the bandstand so the barbecue-eating contestants could listen to "The Washington Post March" while they ate. Although Rhodes liked marches, they weren't exactly his idea of music to aid digestion.

He sat down at the table in a metal folding chair that had been so hot from standing in the sun that it almost took the hide off his rear end. There was a stack of paper napkins in front of him, and after unfolding one and tucking it into his shirt collar, he used another to mop some of the sweat off his face.

"You ought not to do that," Ivy said. "You're going to need that napkin later."

"I needed it now," Rhodes said.

Jennifer Loam walked up.

"Are you going for the championship?" she asked.

"I think I have a chance," Rhodes told her.

Jay Beaman came up and said, "Don't count on it. Nobody's been able to beat me yet."

Jennifer ignored him, and he sat down by Rhodes. He was still wearing the same cap he'd worn the previous day. Or maybe he'd never taken it off.

"Ee-yow!" he said. "That chair's hot!"

"The barbecue might be even hotter," Rhodes said.

"I didn't know you were a big eater, Sheriff," Beaman said, tucking a napkin in his collar as Rhodes had done.

"I'm not," Rhodes said.

Ivy laughed. "Not unless he gets a chance."

The band stopped playing, and Jennifer moved away from the table. There was scattered applause for the band, and Vernell Lindsey went to a microphone on the bandstand. It whistled and shrieked when she tried to talk, but someone finally got it adjusted. First she thanked the Clearview High School Catamount Marching Band for the music, and then she explained the rules of the rib-eating contest. The rules were fairly simple: the rib bones had to be cleaned.

"No leaving meat all over them," Vernell said. "The person with the most bones piled up at the end of fifteen minutes is the winner."

"You don't have a chance," Beaman told Rhodes, and the band started playing again, a repeat of "El Capitan."

The barbecuers brought paper plates heaped with ribs to the table. They set them down, and Rhodes started eating. The different kinds of sauce were all so tangy that after a few minutes his mouth was seared on the inside and he couldn't distinguish one from the other.

There was a glass of ice water by the plate where he was piling the bones, but Rhodes didn't want to take time to drink. Beaman was already pulling ahead. In fact, he'd eaten nearly twice as many ribs as Rhodes had, and the contest had hardly gotten started.

By the time Ralph Oliver brought the last little plate of ribs and set it down by Beaman, Rhodes knew that he'd lost. Jay Beaman was going to be the undisputed champion unless there was someone down at the end of the table who'd eaten more. Rhodes didn't see how that could be possible. He pushed his plate aside and drank the whole glass of water.

"I knew you didn't have a chance, Sheriff," Beaman said. He threw down the last rib bone onto the plate and licked his fingers. Then he belched lightly into a napkin. "You're just an amateur when it comes to eating."

"You're right," Rhodes said, deciding it was time to push Beaman a little and see what happened. He looked around at the crowd that had gathered to encourage them in their endeavors. "But you must be a little disappointed. I don't see your personal cheerleader here."

Beaman's face was covered in drying barbecue sauce, and he was busily wiping his fingers with the paper napkins.

"What personal cheerleader?" he said.

"Linda Fenton," Rhodes said. "You remember her, don't you?"

Beaman threw the napkins on the table and said, "I told you yesterday I didn't know her. I still don't."

"She was clerking at one of your fireworks stands yesterday," Rhodes said. "She's driving a pickup registered in your name. She was at your house last night. So I think you know her, all right."

"Fireworks stands?" Beaman said. "I don't know what you're talking about."

"Sure you do. And so will the rest of the county when I tell Jennifer Loam about them."

"You bastard," Beaman said.

He stood up, kicking his metal chair back and away from him. It landed with a clang, and Beaman grabbed Rhodes by the shoulder.

"Get up," Beaman said.

People all around were looking and pointing.

They couldn't hear what was being said because the band was so loud, but they knew something entertaining was about to happen.

Rhodes stood up and said, "I think Grat Bilson knew about the fireworks. I think he was going to tell the reporter."

He might have said more, but that was when Beaman hit him.

24

Rhodes stumbled backward and fell against the table, which collapsed beneath him. Bones and barbecue sauce scattered in all directions, with plenty of both landing on Rhodes. He could feel the sauce soaking into his clothes.

He didn't have time to feel much else because Beaman took hold of his shirt front and pulled him to his feet. He would have hit Rhodes again, but Rhodes didn't give him a chance. Rhodes hit first, slamming Beaman in the stomach with a right and then a left.

Beaman sagged and let go of Rhodes's shirt. Rhodes just had time to think *big, but soft* when Beaman stood up to his full height. It would have been an imposing sight even if Beaman hadn't been holding the metal chair in both hands.

"Fight fair!" someone yelled.

Rhodes wondered who it was. Maybe it was Ivy.

"Yeah," someone else called out. "This ain't the pro rasslin'."

Beaman didn't seem to care about fighting fair, or maybe he just wasn't listening. He swung the chair like a club.

There wasn't much Rhodes could do except try to take most of the force of the blow on the arm and side. Luckily for Rhodes, Beaman hit him with the flat of the chair instead of the edge, which might have caused real damage.

It caused enough damage as it was, knocking Rhodes sideways into another chair. He tangled with the chair for a second and then fell down on the collapsed table.

A voice from the crowd called out, "Somebody call the law!"

"That's the law that's gettin' the hell beat out of him, you dumb-ass," someone replied.

Beaman still had hold of the chair, and he was advancing on Rhodes with it held high over his head. In the background Rhodes could hear what he always thought of as the "web-footed duck" section of "Stars and Stripes Forever."

The show must go on, he thought, and wondered if anyone would come to his rescue.

No one did.

Beaman brought the chair down in a blur of motion, and Rhodes rolled out of the way. The chair smashed into the table with a loud crack. Rib bones, paper plates, and plastic utensils bounced up into the air and fell back down.

Rhodes stood up, but he put his foot into a puddle of sauce on the table and slipped right back down.

"I'll get you this time," Beaman said, swinging the chair up over his head for another swat.

Rhodes saw Ivy run out of the crowd behind

Beaman. She jumped up, grabbed one leg of the chair, and pulled down with all her strength. She was no match for Beaman, but she did surprise him and throw him off balance.

When he turned to see who was behind him, Rhodes got into a crouch and ran at him.

Beaman let go of the chair and stood like a stone pillar, his arms stretched wide. Rhodes stopped while he was still a couple of feet away. He didn't want to get into a hugging contest with Beaman, who would crush him like an aluminum can.

"Shoot him, Sheriff," someone yelled.

Rhodes had his pistol, or he thought he still had it. He wasn't going to reach for it and find out. He wasn't going to shoot anyone.

While Beaman was eyeing Rhodes, Ivy swung the folding chair and whacked Beaman in the back of the head with it.

It clanged against his cap but didn't appear to bother Beaman much. He just turned around and grabbed the chair, yanking it from Ivy's hand as if she were a five-year-old.

Rhodes took a step forward, but Beaman wheeled back around, swinging the chair through the air so fast that it whistled.

It was then that Rhodes realized that the band had stopped playing and the crowd had grown very quiet. It was as if they had all stopped breathing while they waited for Beaman to finish Rhodes off.

Beaman didn't seem to think he'd need the chair to do it. He tossed it aside and advanced on Rhodes.

Rhodes waited for him to get close enough, then kicked him in the knee.

Beaman's knee didn't crack, but he was hurt. He said, "I wish you hadn't done that, Sheriff. You're about to make me mad."

"I wouldn't want to do that," Rhodes said. "It's still not too late for you to give up."

Beaman laughed. "You always did have a sense of humor, Rhodes."

"If you stop now, I won't file charges on you for this. We can go to the jail where it's air-conditioned, and you can answer a few questions for me."

Beaman wiped a hand across his forehead and flicked sweat drops to the ground.

"What's the matter, Rhodes? You scared of taking a beating?"

"I don't think I'll have to take anything," Rhodes said, and kicked Beaman in the other knee.

Beaman bent over this time, and Rhodes gave him a hard open-handed slap across the chops, snapping Beaman's head to the left and bloodying his mouth.

Beaman spit blood, smiled with his split lips, and hit Rhodes in the chest with a fist like a sledge.

Rhodes stumbled backward across the table and into the stone wall of the bandstand. Beaman followed him, still smiling, trampling rib bones under his feet.

Was having your back to the wall supposed to be good or bad? Rhodes couldn't remember, but he was pretty sure that in his situation it was bad.

Beaman aimed a bucket-sized fist at Rhodes's head. Rhodes saw it coming and ducked away at the last second. The fist struck the wall.

Rhodes thought he heard small bones break and decided that having your back to the wall wasn't so bad. He managed to get a few swift blows into Beaman's soft stomach before Beaman straightened again.

Beaman's right arm dangled at his side, and Rhodes thought that his hand must be hurting quite a bit. Beaman wasn't smiling anymore, either.

But he wasn't quitting, either. He swung at Rhodes with his left hand, and Rhodes wasn't quite fast enough to get out of the way. Beaman's fist nearly took his ear off.

Rhodes backed along the side of the bandstand, kicking paper plates aside, trying to get a firm footing.

Beaman also seemed to be having trouble standing upright. There was an odd look in his eyes, as if he were puzzled about something, though Rhodes couldn't figure out what it might be. He opened his mouth as if he were about to say something, then closed it and swung again.

Rhodes was ready this time, and for some reason Beaman's fist wasn't traveling as fast as it had earlier. Rhodes grabbed Beaman's arm, pulling the big man forward.

Beaman couldn't hold himself back, and Rhodes forced the arm down, turning Beaman's head in the direction of the bandstand wall.

The cap cushioned the crash a little, Rhodes thought, but Beaman's head met the wall with a satisfying thud. Beaman fell and didn't move. Some of the red, white, and blue bunting drifted down and rested on him.

Rhodes reached down and picked up a napkin that didn't have too much sauce on it. He was wiping his face when Ivy got to him.

"I wish you wouldn't get into fights," she said. "I was afraid he was going to kill you."

"I didn't expect him to get violent," Rhodes said. "Thanks for the help, by the way."

"I didn't do much."

"You did enough," Rhodes said.

He looked down at Beaman who still hadn't moved. Rhodes turned his gaze to the crowd and spotted Dr. White among the spectators.

"Better come over here and have a look at him," Rhodes called over the excited talk that had broken out.

Dr. White walked over and knelt down by Beaman. He tried to turn the big man over, but Beaman was too heavy.

Something in Dr. White's expression bothered Rhodes, who started to kneel down beside him. White waved Rhodes away and moved some of the bunting aside. He put his hand to Beaman's neck. The crowd grew quiet again.

After a few seconds, White looked up at Rhodes and shook his head.

"Jesus Christ," someone yelled. "The sheriff's killed Jay Beaman!"

25

Rhodes didn't go to the historical pageant that afternoon, but he was sure that it must have been anticlimactic for any of the people who had witnessed his fight with Jay Beaman. They were still talking after the ambulance had come and taken Beaman to Ballinger's, and unless Rhodes missed his guess, they'd be talking about it for months.

He didn't blame them. It wasn't often you got to see the David and Goliath story reenacted on the Fourth of July to the accompaniment of Sousa marches. Of course he'd used a rock wall instead of a smooth, flat river rock, but it was all the same to the crowd.

But Rhodes wasn't sure that what happened had anything to do with David and Goliath. David had killed Goliath, and Rhodes didn't believe he'd killed Beaman.

Beaman might have hit the wall hard enough to knock himself out, though Rhodes wasn't sure even of that.

The man from the radio station had been sure, however. He'd come running over from the sound truck, stuck a mike in Rhodes's face, and said, "How does it feel to kill a man, Sheriff?"

Rhodes said he didn't know, that he'd never killed anyone, but the announcer didn't want to let it go. Rhodes had finally told him that he'd withhold judgment on what had happened until the autopsy report and walked away. There was no telling what the announcer might have said after that, and Rhodes didn't even want to know.

When he'd gotten the crowd quieted down, he drove to Ballinger's to have a talk with Dr. White, who had ridden in the ambulance along with Beaman's body.

"How complete an autopsy do you do when you think you already know the cause of death?" Rhodes asked.

"Are you trying to insult me, Sheriff?" White said.

They were in Ballinger's office, and Ballinger was watching them as they talked. He'd been reading a book, as usual, but he'd put it down. Rhodes couldn't quite read the title on the cover, or maybe he could. It appeared to be *The Spy with the Blue Kazoo*, though Rhodes didn't see how that could be right. What kind of title was that?

"Dr. White always does a complete job," Ballinger said. "You know that."

"Yes," Rhodes said. "I do know that."

He felt dirty and gritty and uncomfortable, and there was a big wet stain on his shirt from the barbecue sauce. He didn't feel like getting into an argument.

"Then why were you asking?" Dr. White wanted to know.

"Because I thought that in a routine autopsy there might be some things you might not check for."

"If he had a heart attack or a stroke, I'll find out," Dr. White said.

"Good," Rhodes said, relieved. "Because I think that must be what killed him. He got a funny look on his face while we were fighting, as if something might be worrying him. He didn't hit his head very hard, either. I just don't see how he could have died from it."

"You never know about head injuries," Dr. White said, and Rhodes began to feel bad again. "Sometimes even the tiniest blow in just the right place is enough to cause death. But don't worry. I'll find out."

"He was pretty big and out of shape," Ballinger said. "I'd bet on the heart attack."

"That's not exactly scientific," Dr. White told him. "I'll do a thorough job. You can count on it."

"Thanks," Rhodes said.

Rhodes went by his house to bathe and change clothes.

"You're beginning to make a habit of this," Ivy said when he came out of the bathroom.

"I didn't intend to," Rhodes said. "I cleaned the tub again, too."

"That's a habit I like," Ivy said. "And I like your decorations, by the way."

201

Rhodes twisted around to look at his back and side. The bruises from where Beaman had hit him with the chair were beginning to turn dark.

"It's going to look even more colorful to-morrow," he said.

"It's probably going to hurt more, too."

"I think I can count on that," Rhodes said.

Ivy had left the door to the bedroom open, and Yancey charged into the room and yipped around Rhodes, now and then taking a nip at his bare ankles as Rhodes tried to get dressed.

"I'm going to feed you to Speedo if you keep it up," Rhodes told the dog.

"You shouldn't talk like that," Ivy told him. "You'll scare the poor thing."

Rhodes reached down to put his socks on, and Yancey barked at his hand.

"I can see he's terrified," Rhodes said.

Ivy picked up the little dog and carried him into another room. When she came back to the bedroom, she shut the door. In under two seconds, Yancey was yapping outside, but Ivy and Rhodes ignored him.

"I can't believe that man died today," Ivy said. "I didn't think it was possible to kill someone like that."

Rhodes had wondered when she'd bring the subject up. He said, "I don't think I killed him. I think it was something else."

"What could it have been? I heard his head hit that wall."

"It hit the wall, all right, but not hard enough

to kill him. Maybe he had a heart attack. Or an aneurysm, something like that."

"Do you really think so?"

"I really do."

"Good. I don't like thinking that you had anything to do with it."

Rhodes didn't like thinking that either. He said, "Did you stay at the park long after I left?"

"About ten minutes. I think you and Beaman might have put a damper on the rib-eating contest."

"Did they go on and have the judging of the barbecue?"

"I think so. Your friend James Allen was one of the judges. That man from the radio station was going around talking to all the cooks about their methods."

"But you didn't stick around to see who won?"

"I wasn't very interested. Jennifer Loam was there because she had to write about it for the paper, but I could tell she was just itching to get started on her story about the brawling, two-fisted sheriff of Blacklin County."

"That sounds like it should be on a poster for an old black-and-white movie," Rhodes said. "Starring Allan 'Rocky' Lane, or maybe 'Wild Bill' Elliott."

"Who are they?"

"Cowboy stars."

"I'm not old enough to remember them, I guess."

"Me neither," Rhodes said. "But I've seen their movies on TV. They're sort of like those books Clyde Ballinger likes, short and to the point. Do we have any Tums around here?"

"Getting too old to eat spicy foods?" Ivy asked.

"It's not that I'm too old," Rhodes said. "It's just that I shouldn't exercise right after eating."

"I'll look in the bathroom cabinet," Ivy said.

"Don't let the dog in," Rhodes told her, but it was too late. As soon as Ivy opened the door, Yancey shot through the crack and attacked Rhodes's feet.

"You should surrender," Ivy said.

"Good idea," Rhodes said. "Do you think he'll notice?"

"Probably not," Ivy said.

When Rhodes arrived at the jail, Hack and Lawton were waiting, and Rhodes knew what they wanted to hear.

So he said, "Anything happen today?"

"You know what happened," Hack said. "You were in on it. We want to hear about it. I know there's more to it than was on the radio."

Usually the pair would never have admitted their eagerness. Rhodes smiled and said, "On the radio? Something was on the radio?"

"You know what it was," Lawton said. "All about how you killed Jay Beaman in a fistfight."

"I said I didn't kill him. On the radio."

"Yeah, but that's not the way it sounded from

the way the guy told it," Hack said. "It sounded like you beat Beaman to a pulp and then rammed his head into the wall."

"That's not exactly the way it happened," Rhodes said. "In the first place, I didn't kill anybody. I'm pretty sure Beaman must've had a heart attack. And if anyone was getting beaten to a pulp, it was me. Beaman hit me with a chair. I have the bruises to prove it."

"Must've been quite a fight, then," Hack said.

"It was more of a fight than I wanted it to be."

"What started it?" Lawton asked.

"I mentioned Beaman's ex-convict friend. I should have kept my mouth shut."

"You're gonna get a lot of publicity out of it," Hack said.

"But it's not good publicity," Rhodes said. "I don't like to be thought of as a killer."

"Maybe the story in the newspaper will be better," Hack said.

"What story?"

"The one that reporter's gonna write."

"I haven't talked to her," Rhodes said. "So she can't write a story."

"Sure she can," Lawton said. "She called a while ago. She's probably on her way here right now to interview you."

Just what I need, Rhodes thought. He said, "Has Ruth called in lately? Any word on Beaman's friend?"

"No calls," Hack said. "But Ruth had an idea. She's on her way to Thurston to check it out."

"What's the idea?" Rhodes asked.

Hack shrugged. "She didn't say."

"But she'll let you know if she runs into trouble."

"You bet," Hack said.

26

Rhodes sat at his desk, patiently answering Jennifer Loam's questions, while Hack and Lawton pretended that they were too busy to be listening in on the conversation.

Rhodes repeated his theory that Beaman had died of a heart attack or some other physical problem and told the reporter that he hoped she'd put that into her story.

"I can't just speculate on the cause of death," she said. "I'd have to have proof."

"You don't have to speculate," Rhodes told her. "I'll do that. I think your readers should know that I didn't kill anybody."

Jennifer said she'd put Rhodes's idea about the death into the story. Then she asked him about Linda Fenton.

"Nobody's seen her," Rhodes said. "But one of the deputies is working on a theory."

"What theory?"

Since Rhodes didn't know the answer to the question, he said, "It's confidential."

He thought he heard Hack choke back a laugh, and Jennifer turned to look at the dispatcher. But Hack showed no sign of having made a sound.

"I guess you're a little upset that Beaman's dead," Rhodes said to distract Jennifer.

"I'm always upset when someone dies," she said. "But I didn't like Mr. Beaman very much."

"Now there's no way you can ever finish your big story about the county government."

"You never know," Jennifer said.

"It would be hard," Rhodes said, "what with both the principals dead."

He thought about that for a second. The two men involved in her story were both dead, and she'd had contact with both of them. Was there anyone else who had? He wondered if she might have a motive for wanting Bilson dead.

"I don't like the way you're looking at me," Jennifer said. "You aren't thinking I had anything to do with Mr. Bilson's murder, I hope."

Rhodes didn't want to tell her the truth, so he said, "No. I was just thinking that it's funny that both he and Beaman are dead now."

"I don't think it's funny."

"I didn't mean it as a joke. I meant it was strange."

"There's nothing strange about the way Beaman died. You broke his head open."

"You know that's not true," Rhodes said.

"Yes. I'm sorry. I just don't like being treated like a suspect."

"You're not a suspect," Rhodes said, but he wasn't so sure about that.

Hack's radio crackled at that moment, and

Rhodes heard Ruth Grady's voice. The deputy had found Linda Fenton. She was in Jay Beaman's house in Thurston.

"Tell her not to do anything," Rhodes said to Hack. "I'll be there in twenty minutes."

"What about our interview?" Jennifer asked.

"We'll finish it later," Rhodes said.

Since Thurston was a little over twenty miles from Clearview, Rhodes didn't pay much attention to the speed limit on his way there. He was careful, but he kept the accelerator pressed down. What bothered him was that every time he looked in the mirror, he saw Jennifer Loam's little car behind him. It seemed as if the reporter was following him everywhere he went. She was turning into a pest. Rhodes knew that she was just doing her job as she saw fit, but he didn't like the idea of civilians being involved in his business, story or no story.

When he arrived in Thurston, he found Ruth Grady parked in the same deserted service station where she'd been the previous night. This time it was still broad daylight, so Rhodes got a good look at Beaman's house. It looked even shabbier than it had in the darkness.

"Is she still in there?" Rhodes asked Ruth.

Before she even had time to answer, Jennifer Loam's car pulled up beside them.

"Who's that?" Ruth asked.

"Jennifer Loam. The reporter."

"What's she doing here?"

"She followed me. Just a minute."

He walked over to Jennifer's car and tapped on the window. Jennifer rolled it down and Rhodes said, "You can watch from here, but don't get out of the car. Understand?"

Jennifer nodded, and Rhodes went back to Ruth's car.

"What about Linda Fenton?" he asked.

"She's in the house."

"How did you find her?"

"I just thought that she might show up here. If she heard that Beaman was dead, and if she left anything in his house, she'd want to get it."

"Good thinking," Rhodes said, wishing he'd thought of it himself. Considering Fenton's background, Rhodes thought that she might even decide to take along a few things that she hadn't left. "Was she here when you got here, or did she come later?"

"She was already here."

"Where's the pickup?"

"In back."

Rhodes thought about that. He hated to say anything, but Fenton had gotten out the back last night. What was to stop her from doing the same thing again?

"I let the air out of the tires," Ruth said.

"What?"

"I let the air —"

"I heard you. It just seems that women are reading my mind these days."

"I wasn't reading your mind. I just knew you'd be wondering about that. Anyway, she's not going anywhere."

"Good. I'll go have a little visit with her."

"You want me to go along?"

"You can wait here. I'll let you know if I need you. And keep an eye on the reporter."

"I'll do that," Ruth said.

Rhodes didn't know why he thought Linda Fenton would come to the door. If he'd thought about it, he'd have known she'd just stay inside and keep right on doing whatever it was that she was doing. It wasn't her house, after all. As far as Rhodes was concerned, she didn't have any business being there in the first place, much less answering the door. But she probably saw things differently.

Rhodes tried the door, and the knob turned in his hand. He wasn't surprised. Hardly anyone in a town like Thurston bothered locking the door. There hadn't been a major crime there in quite a while, and only a few minor ones. Not counting armadillo hunters.

Rhodes went into the house, which looked just as cluttered as it had the last time he'd seen it. There was no one lurking about in the front room, but he could hear someone moving around upstairs.

The house had been cool on Rhodes's last visit, but it wasn't cool now. The air conditioner was turned off, and the place was hot and stuffy.

And dusty. Beaman probably hadn't dusted in years. Rhodes took a breath, and it was like breathing through cloth.

He went up the stairs. When he reached the top, he looked down the hallway. The door to one room was open. Rhodes stood where he was and said, "This is the sheriff. Come on out, Ms. Fenton."

The noise in the room stopped, but no one came out. No one said anything, either.

"Ms. Fenton?" Rhodes said.

Still no answer. Rhodes walked down the hallway to the door, but he didn't show himself to the person in the room. He was beginning to have a bad feeling about things. He drew his pistol.

"Ms. Fenton?" he said.

He heard something, but it wasn't a reply. It was the sound of a window being opened.

He stepped into the doorway, his pistol close to his body, and said, "Stop right there."

Linda Fenton was halfway out the window.

"I thought all you cops said *freeze*," she said.

"Maybe they do on TV," Rhodes said. "I wouldn't know. I don't watch much TV. Come on back in. You're just going to fall and hurt yourself if you try to go out that way. This is the second floor, after all."

Linda came back into the room. She turned and looked at Rhodes.

"There's a back-porch roof right under this window. I wouldn't fall too far."

"You still might hurt yourself. I wouldn't want that to happen."

"Why not?"

"I need some information from you."

Linda looked at Rhodes and for the first time seemed to recognize him.

"I remember you," she said. "You're the guy from the fireworks stand."

"The sheriff," Rhodes said.

"Kinda cute, for a sheriff. Most lawmen I've been around looked more like the back end of a horse."

Flattery from an arsonist, Rhodes thought, putting a hand to his hair. Maybe it wasn't thinning, after all.

"We need to have a talk," he said, looking around the room. There was a rumpled bed, a dresser, and a small night table. There was a pillow on the bed, but it didn't have a pillowcase. The case was on the floor, and it looked lumpy. Rhodes figured it was full of things that Linda had taken from the dresser and night table.

"All that stuff belongs to me, you know?" Linda said.

"What stuff?"

"The stuff in the pillowcase."

Rhodes was really getting tired of women who could read his mind. He said, "I'm sure it's your stuff. But I might have to check it out anyway."

"Go ahead. Doesn't matter to me. If you're not embarrassed, I won't be, either."

Rhodes wondered what might be in the pillowcase. He figured he could find out later.

"Let's just leave it there right now," he said. "We can go downstairs and talk."

"Fine with me. You don't need that gun, though. I'll go quietly."

Rhodes holstered the pistol and gestured to the doorway.

"After you," he said.

27

Linda Fenton's story was that she had been saved by the Texas Department of Criminal Justice.

"I stopped smoking, for one thing, you know?" she said. "Smoking gives you wrinkles, and it's not good for your health, but I was smoking two packs a day when I went in the joint. You wouldn't believe how much tobacco costs in that place since they made it illegal. So I quit smoking. Look at this face." She put a hand to her cheek. "Smooth as a baby's butt. You'd never guess how old I am."

Rhodes wasn't going to fall into that trap. He said, "Probably not."

"Damn right. Anyway, just stopping smoking didn't solve all my problems. People don't trust you if you're a con. Just because you burned down a building, they think you might do it again, or do something even worse. Not the ones in the pen with you, but everybody else. I wanted to meet some people in the free world who wouldn't treat me like dirt, so I put my picture up on that Web site to see what would happen. Jay Beaman wrote me a letter."

Linda had turned on the air conditioner, but

215

the atmosphere in the room was still close. Rhodes looked around. The empty beer can was still on the coffee table, along with the half-full (or half-empty) glass of water and the ashtray. Rhodes would have been more comfortable at the jail, but he didn't think Linda would feel the same way.

"Did Jay tell you he was a county commissioner?" Rhodes asked.

"In his very first letter. He said that meant we'd have to keep our relationship secret, you know? I let him know right off the bat that we didn't have any relationship, and he wrote back that he hoped we might develop one. And would you believe it? We did."

"It wasn't a very good idea," Rhodes said. "It would have hurt him in the election if people found out."

"Nobody was going to find out. We were going to be careful. I wasn't even living in this county."

"I know. I would've been notified if you had been."

"I did work at his fireworks stand, which I guess was a mistake, but it gave me something to do."

"I didn't know he owned those stands until today," Rhodes said.

"That was another one of his secrets, not that there was anything wrong with owning them. It was a way to make money, you know? Commissioners don't make all that much in salary in

216

this county. But he said some people wouldn't understand about that, so the stands were his little secret."

"Some of his fellow commissioners wouldn't understand," Rhodes said, thinking of James Allen. "That's for sure."

"Well, it doesn't matter much now, you know? I really hate it that you killed Jay. He was one of the few people who was nice to me."

"I didn't kill him," Rhodes said.

"Right. All you did was bust his head."

Rhodes was tired of explaining his theory of how Beaman had died. He said, "Speaking of people being killed, Mrs. Bilson was pretty upset with you yesterday afternoon."

"She's a crazy woman," Linda said. "Jay told me about her. He never should've gotten mixed up with her, he said. It wasn't his idea, anyway. It was hers. He got tired of her pretty fast."

"Her husband was murdered the other night," Rhodes said. "His body was found after a house burned down."

"I heard about that. I didn't burn the house down, though, if that's what you're thinking."

"I was thinking that he was investigating Jay Beaman and that he'd found out a lot of things about him that Beaman might not want anyone to know."

"If you mean me, you're right. He didn't want anybody to know about the two of us. But he didn't have anything else to hide." She paused. "Well, there were the fireworks stands. But aside from me and the stands, he didn't care what people knew about him."

Rhodes didn't think Jay Beaman would have been crazy enough to discuss all his business dealings, legal or illegal, with an ex-convict. In fact, if he'd had any sense at all, he would've been especially careful not to mention anything illegal. It wouldn't have been logical for Beaman to have trusted Linda that much. On the other hand, it wasn't logical for him to be involved with her in the first place, so he might have told her quite a bit.

"Did he ever mention Grat Bilson to you?" Rhodes asked.

"The dead man? Sure. He told me that Bilson was snooping around. He was jealous because Jay had been seeing his wife. What a dope, you know? From what Jay told me, everybody in the county had been seeing that woman."

"Not everybody," Rhodes said.

"Well, nearly everybody. Anyway, her husband was always coming around the precinct barn, talking to the workers, trying to get them to tell him stuff. Jay said he didn't have any right to be bothering the workers like that, so naturally he tried to put a stop to it."

Rhodes thought it would also be natural to put a stop to it if there was something Beaman didn't want his workers talking about.

"What about bribes?" Rhodes asked.

"Bribes? Jay didn't ever say anything to me about any bribes. Not that it would be any of my business. It's not like we were gonna get married or anything, you know? But he treated me like a decent woman, which is more than I can say for most people. Anyway, I don't think he took bribes. Would he be living in a crummy place like this if he had money?"

Rhodes was having a hard time deciding how much of Linda's line to believe, but she had a point about the bribes. Maybe she was telling the truth about everything. Against his will, Rhodes found himself believing her.

He warned himself that people who have been in prison are often very convincing liars, but he wasn't sure that Linda had any reason to lie.

"Jay and I liked to watch TV in here," Linda said, looking around the untidy room. "Sometimes we'd have popcorn."

Rhodes found it hard to imagine Jay Beaman and Linda Fenton as a domestic pair, sitting on the couch, their feet propped up on the coffee table while they watched *N.Y.P.D. Blue* and ate popcorn out of a plastic bowl, but he supposed that was possible, like everything else Linda had told him. If Beaman didn't have anything to hide, though, why had he gotten so upset when Rhodes mentioned Linda at the rib-eating contest? Was it simply because he didn't want his little secret to get out and have some effect on his next election campaign?

"Sitting here, it's almost like he was in the room, you know?" Linda said. "I just can't believe he's gone."

Rhodes thought for a second that she might start crying, but she didn't. She said, "Look over there. See that shadow? It could be Jay."

Rhodes turned to see what shadow she might be talking about. He didn't see anything except the TV set. He was about to say so, but something very hard slammed into the back of his head. He tried to stand up, but he couldn't feel his legs, and then he couldn't feel anything at all.

28

It was raining. Rhodes could feel the water dripping onto his face, and he wondered how he'd gotten outside.

He opened his eyes and got a blurry view of Beaman's living room. The view was a bit skewed because Rhodes was lying on the floor. Jennifer Loam was dripping water onto his face from the glass on the coffee table.

Rhodes started to sit up, but a sharp pain threatened to split his skull right down the middle. So he stayed where he was.

"Are you okay?" Jennifer said.

Rhodes said that, no, he wasn't okay. Or that's what he thought he said. From the look of concern on Jennifer's blurred face, he might not have made much sense.

"You really don't look so good," Jennifer said.

Rhodes tried again to sit up. The pain wasn't as bad this time, and he was able to lean against the chair he'd been sitting in. He put a hand to the back of his head and felt a sticky, tender knot.

His vision was improving, and he noticed that the ashtray from the coffee table was lying on the floor nearby. He knew whose fingerprints would be on it. He wiped water off his face and thought about how he'd been conned.

"I think someone hit you," Jennifer said. "I think you might have a concussion."

Rhodes didn't agree about the concussion. He had a headache, but his vision was fine again. He even thought he might be able to stand up, so he gave it a try.

He was a little wobbly, but he didn't fall down. He said, "Where's Linda Fenton?"

"Gone. Is she the one who hit you?"

"Yes. With that ashtray over there. Where's she gone?"

"I don't know. Deputy Grady and I were sitting in our cars, and we saw a pickup come driving out from behind the house. We were really surprised."

Rhodes was surprised, too. He said, "I thought Ruth let the air out of the tires."

"She did. That's why we were so surprised. But the tires were okay when we saw the truck. I think Mr. Beaman must've had some of those little cans of flat-fixer in his truck."

Rhodes hadn't thought about that possibility, but it made sense. Beaman was in charge of a lot of vehicles at the precinct barn, and he would have learned that it paid to be prepared for emergencies like flat tires. It would have taken Linda only a few seconds to inflate the truck tires at least partially with the cans of compressed air and gunk that stopped up any little holes.

"Where's Ruth?" Rhodes asked.

"She told me to come see about you, and she went after the truck."

Rhodes tried walking a few steps. He was steadier than he'd thought he would be. He was fine, in fact, except for being embarrassed at having let Linda get the better of him. And except for a little buzzing in his head.

"Which way did they go?" he asked.

"Out of town."

"I know this is a small town, but there's more than one way out of it."

"I'm directionally challenged," Jennifer said. "I can never tell north from south. Or east from west, for that matter."

Rhodes pointed in the direction of Clearview and said, "That's north."

Jennifer pointed to his right. "Then which way would that be?"

"That would be east."

"They went east," Jennifer said.

"Thanks," Rhodes said, and started to leave. But then he thought better of it and went back upstairs. The pillowcase was still on the floor of the bedroom.

When he bent over to pick it up, Rhodes felt another pain shoot through his head, but it wasn't severe. He straightened up, and the pain was gone again.

Jennifer Loam watched him from the doorway as he set the pillowcase on the bed and started going through it.

He discovered, to his surprise, that Linda hadn't lied about the contents. Everything seemed quite likely to belong to her. There was some makeup, some skimpy undergarments, a pair of jeans, and a couple of shirts. The only suspicious item was a small Bose radio/CD player located at the bottom of the pillowcase. Rhodes doubted that it belonged to Linda, but maybe it did.

"What is all that stuff?" Jennifer asked.

"Some of Linda Fenton's belongings," Rhodes said. "She was gathering them up when I got here."

"Why did she leave them?"

"I imagine she was in a hurry to get away."

"And why did she hit you?"

"Probably because she thought I was going to arrest her instead of sending her on her way. I got the feeling she didn't like jail very much."

"Were you?"

"Was I what?"

"Going to arrest her."

"I don't know," Rhodes said. "I didn't have any real reason to. I just wanted to find out some things from her."

"Did you?" Jennifer said. "Find out some things, I mean."

"I found out it wasn't a good idea to turn my back on her," Rhodes said.

When he got to the county car, Rhodes called Ruth on the radio and found out that she was in the area around the big lake in the southeastern part of the county.

"I think I lost her," Ruth said.

Rhodes wasn't surprised at the news. There were all kinds of little roads around the lake, most of them unpaved, and they wound among the trees and cabins for miles and miles of lakeshore.

"I'm sorry, Sheriff," Ruth said. "I guess I should have slashed those tires instead of just letting the air out."

"You don't want to go committing misdemeanors," Rhodes said.

"I'm just mad at myself. She could be in Mexico by tomorrow."

"I'm as much at fault as anybody," Rhodes said. "I let my guard down, and she conked me. That's the only reason she got away."

"Are you all right?"

"I'm fine. My pride is hurt, that's all."

"I'm going to keep looking. She could have pulled into a driveway at one of the lake houses, or maybe she drove off into the trees."

The mention of the lake houses gave Rhodes an idea. He said, "Call Hack. Have him find out if Beaman had a lake house. If he did, you can check it out."

"Good idea," Ruth said, and signed off.

"You think she'll find her?" Jennifer Loam asked.

She was standing by the car, having listened in to Rhodes's side of the entire conversation.

"You never know," Rhodes said.

"Will it make any difference if she does catch her?"

Rhodes wasn't sure whether it would or not, so he just shrugged.

"Let's see," Ivy said as she dabbed the back of Rhodes's head with some kind of strong-smelling antibiotic. "You're been hit by a folding chair and a few fists, killed a man, and been swatted with an ashtray. That's a pretty impressive list of accomplishments for one day. And it's only been dark for about half an hour."

She didn't sound pleased, so Rhodes thought his best defense was to say nothing at all. He wanted to remind her that he hadn't killed anyone, but he thought that some other time might be better.

"At least you don't need any stitches," Ivy went on. "That's about the best I can say for you. I don't know how much longer you can go on getting yourself beaten up like this. Why don't you take up a more sensible profession, like alligator wrestling?"

Rhodes kept his mouth shut. If he could have thought of a clever retort, he would have made it, but he couldn't come up with anything.

"I don't think there's any need for a bandage," Ivy said. "It would just get all messed up in your hair, anyway. Of course I could shave the back of your head if you really want a bandage. What do you think?"

"Um," Rhodes said.

Being noncommittal had worked so far, and he wasn't going to risk changing tactics.

"I don't think you should run for office again," Ivy said, the tone of her voice leaving Rhodes no doubt that she meant it.

He decided that he'd better speak up. He said, "I have to run again. Who else would put up with Hack and Lawton?"

"Don't try to be funny," Ivy said. "You know how I feel about this."

It was a discussion they'd had once or twice before. Ivy didn't like the risks Rhodes took. She really believed it was time for him to find a different line of work.

Rhodes didn't feel that way at all. He couldn't imagine what the different kind of work could possibly be. Being a greeter at Wal-Mart? Grilling burgers at McDonald's?

"You could run for commissioner," Ivy said. "There's an opening."

"I don't think that would look good," Rhodes said. "After all, I killed the last man in the office."

"You did not!"

"What? Just a second ago, you said —"

"I don't care what I said. You know I didn't mean it. I was just upset."

Rhodes thought it was time to revert to his former strategy, so he said nothing.

"I'm sorry," Ivy said. "I get upset sometimes. I know you like your job, and I know you're good at it. I don't want you to quit. Well, I do. But you know what I mean."

Rhodes wasn't sure he did know what she meant. He couldn't always follow her logic.

He said, "I don't want to quit. I think I'm doing a good job. But you never know about the voters. They might have a different idea. Maybe they'll find a candidate they like better and retire me at the next election."

"Why would they do that? You're the best sheriff this county ever had."

"Not everyone feels that way."

"Then they're crazy."

"I can never quite figure you out," Rhodes said.

"Good. That's the way I like it. I wouldn't want to be predictable."

"That's something you don't have to worry about."

"Good," Ivy said, "I think that does it for your head. What do you think?"

They were in the bathroom, and Rhodes was sitting in a chair in front of the mirror over the double basin. The door was closed, and Yancey was yipping around outside it. Rhodes could see his own face in the mirror, as well as Ivy's, but he couldn't see the back of his head.

"I can't tell a thing," he said.

Ivy picked up a mirror and held it behind him. Now he could see the back of his head reflected in the mirror in front of him.

"Looks fine to me," he said, though he really couldn't tell a thing about it.

"You're going to have quite a knot. You probably won't be up to any more exercise tonight, what with your back and your head both being messed up."

"What kind of exercise did you have in mind?" Rhodes asked.

Ivy smiled. "Wouldn't you like to know."

"Sure. Go ahead and tell me."

"What's the matter? Don't you like surprises?"

"Sometimes. But only good ones."

"I think you'll like this one, then," Ivy said.

29

The next morning Rhodes sat on a step of the back porch and watched Yancey torment Speedo. Or maybe Speedo was having as much fun as the smaller dog. Rhodes couldn't figure dogs out.

It seemed to Rhodes that it was a little cooler than it had been for a while, but he might have been imagining things. He hadn't seen the weather report the previous night, so he didn't know what the prediction was for the day.

He was feeling fine, though his head was a little sore. He'd had to sleep on his side, and every time he rolled over, the little thrill of pain in his head woke him up. His back and side had caused him a couple of twitches, too, but he thought that as long as he didn't make any sudden moves, he'd be all right.

Rhodes wasn't worried about his head or his back, however, and he wasn't worried about the weather. He was worried about the death of Grat Bilson. He tried to think back over everything that had happened and figure out what he knew about the murder and what he was only supposing.

It turned out on reflection that he didn't know a lot.

Bilson had been hit in the head with a whiskey bottle, or by something. It would be a while before Rhodes got the lab report on the bottle he'd sent away for testing, and even then the report might not be conclusive.

But it was conclusive that Bilson had been hit. It was almost equally certain that someone had started a fire in the hope that the evidence of the murder would be covered up.

That, Rhodes had to admit, was about all he knew for sure. He didn't know whether Yvonne had killed her husband or whether someone else had done it.

If Jay Beaman was the killer, then that would be the end of things, but Rhodes didn't have any evidence to prove that Beaman was the guilty one.

Vernell Lindsey didn't seem to be a likely possibility, though Rhodes still wasn't sure just what her relationship with Bilson had been. That was something he'd probably need to look into more deeply.

As for Linda Fenton, it was likely that she was long gone. Rhodes hadn't gotten a call from Hack, so he assumed that Beaman didn't have a lake house, which meant there was no place that they could look for Fenton unless they could find out where she'd been living.

She'd told Rhodes that she wasn't living in Blacklin County, but it would be easy enough for Rhodes to call the sheriffs of the four surrounding counties and see if she was living in one of them, not that Rhodes expected her to go home and stay there. If she had any sense at all, she'd go to another state, take another name, and live as happily ever after as was possible. Rhodes was sure that she wouldn't be coming back to Blacklin County anytime soon.

But the more he thought about her, the more he thought she might be the one who had killed Bilson. The fireworks stand was close to where the murder had occurred, and she was a convicted arsonist. If she thought Bilson's snooping was a danger to Beaman, the only man who'd treated her like a human being, at least according to her, she might have gone to talk to Grat, gotten angry, and hit him with the bottle. The fire would have been the first thing she thought of when she considered a cover-up.

And if she wasn't guilty of something, why hit Rhodes with the ashtray? Even if he'd taken her to the jail for questioning, he wouldn't have a reason to hold her.

Rhodes stood up. The sudden movement didn't make his head hurt too much. It did cause a little pain in his side, however.

Yancey had located a rubber bone that was one of Speedo's favorite toys and was running around the yard with it in his mouth. Speedo was trying to catch him, but Yancey, while slower than Speedo, was quicker. He eluded him by making sharp stops and turns. Rhodes envied the small dog's agility.

"Come over here, Yancey," Rhodes said, whistling for him. Yancey paid him no mind, but Speedo trotted over to see what Rhodes wanted.

"I was just trying to get your bone back for you," Rhodes said.

Speedo panted and wagged his tail in appreciation of Rhodes's generous nature, or maybe just because that was what he felt like doing at the moment.

Ivy came to the door and called Yancey, who instantly dropped the rubber bone and ran over to the porch.

"Come on in," Ivy said, and Yancey pranced up the steps and went inside.

"I can't figure out how you do that," Rhodes said.

"It's the command voice," Ivy told him. "Some of us have it, some of us don't."

Rhodes didn't think that was it at all, but he knew better than to say so.

"The command voice," he said. "I guess that's it."

Speedo wandered off and located the rubber bone. He brought it over to Rhodes and dropped it at his feet, and gave Rhodes a hopeful look.

Rhodes bent over with only minor discomfort and picked up the bone. Then he threw it to the other side of the yard. Speedo dashed off after it, grabbed it in his mouth, and brought it back. This time he didn't drop it. He waited for Rhodes to reach for it, then backed away.

Rhodes leaned forward and grabbed one end of the bone. Speedo growled and wouldn't let go. Rhodes gave the bone a light shaking, and Speedo planted his feet and tried to pull away. Or pretended to try.

"I don't know who's crazier," Ivy said to Rhodes. "You or those dogs."

"I'd like to think it was the dogs," Rhodes said. "But I wouldn't bet the farm on it."

He let go of the bone, and Speedo's head bobbed up. The dog looked at Rhodes for a second or two, saw Rhodes wasn't going to reach for the bone, and then moved closer. Rhodes made a grab, but Speedo moved his head aside and Rhodes missed. Rhodes laughed, and Speedo looked immensely pleased with himself.

"Crazy or not," Ivy said, "the two of you are certainly alike in one way."

"What way is that?" Rhodes said.

"It takes so little to make you happy."

"You're right about that. Would you say that's a good quality or a bad one?"

"In dogs or men?"

"Either one. Or both."

"Well, I don't know about dogs, but it's a quality I admire in men."

Rhodes made another quick grab for the bone and felt a slight twinge. Speedo danced away.

"How's your back?"

"It's all right. A little sore. But that surprise I got last night took some of the soreness out."

"And what about your head?" Ivy asked.

"It feels fine. I think that antibiotic did the trick. Or the surprise."

"Maybe it was both."

"Could be."

Rhodes stood up. Speedo watched him warily.

"I guess I ought to be going on to work," Rhodes said.

"Actually, that's what I came out here to talk to you about," Ivy said. "Hack called. He said that there was nobody still at work in the courthouse yesterday afternoon when Ruth called him about Beaman having a lake house, so he couldn't find out anything."

"I thought he could just check the phone book," Rhodes said.

"Some people go to the lake to get away from telephones," Ivy said. "Unlike you."

"I don't have a lake house."

"You know what I mean."

Rhodes figured this was another one of those times when he should keep quiet, or at least change the subject. He said, "So does Beaman have a lake house or not?"

"He does. There's no telephone, but Hack knows where it's located. He found out this morning. He said you could either call him or come by the jail and he'd tell you."

"I'll call," Rhodes said.

He went up the steps, but Ivy stood in the door in front of him.

"You'll be careful when you go out there, won't you?"

"I'm always careful," Rhodes said.

"Right. That's why you have a knot the size of a jumbo egg on the back of your head."

"I learned a valuable lesson from that experience," Rhodes said. "I won't turn my back on Linda Fenton again."

"Good. The next time, she might have something more lethal than an ashtray."

"The ashtray was bad enough," Rhodes said.

He looked over his shoulder. Speedo was still standing near the steps, the bone in his mouth.

"Why don't you play with Speedo for me while I make the call," Rhodes said.

Ivy walked down the steps and said, "Speedo, bring me the bone."

Speedo trotted over and dropped the bone at her feet.

Ivy turned to look at Rhodes, smiling.

"Command voice," she said.

30

Rhodes drove down a dusty dirt road near the lake. The leaves of the trees that lined the road were covered with sand stirred up by passing cars. There hadn't been any rain to wash it off, and it clung there, making the leaves look even browner than they were.

The part of the lake where Rhodes was hadn't been developed the way some of the other areas had. There were no little parks with picnic tables, no boat ramps, no fancy houses. If a man wanted to get away from people or his job, or both, this was the place to come.

Rhodes passed a couple of trailers set off in the trees and followed the road around a slight curve that took him to within thirty yards of the water, or where the water should have been. The drought had shrunk the lake considerably. However, if the directions Rhodes had gotten from Hack were right, and if he'd followed them correctly, he should see Beaman's house just about any second.

While it was possible that Linda Fenton might be there, Rhodes didn't have any real hope that she would. She might have spent the night in the house after eluding Ruth, but she was surely gone by now. She had no reason to stay, and plenty of reasons to leave. Ex-convicts who assault police officers usually didn't fare too well with the judges in Blacklin County, and Rhodes was sure that Linda had other reasons for leaving, too.

So he was surprised when he saw Beaman's old pickup parked in front of a ramshackle house that backed up to the shore, or to what had been the shore. The water had retreated at least forty yards into the lake, and there was nothing but mud where it had been, mud with a dry crust on top like that at the stock tank where Rhodes and Yvonne Bilson had had their little tussle. The crust was cracked in a pattern that almost made it look like floor tile.

Rhodes stopped the county car behind the pickup and got out. The air smelled faintly of dead fish and sand. The yard around the house was mostly sand, with a few blades of grass sticking up here and there. It would be a good place to grow watermelons, Rhodes thought. His feet made deep impressions in the sand as he walked over to Beaman's truck to have a look inside.

The window on the driver's side of the truck was rolled down, and the dash was dusty. So was the seat. If the window stayed down, they'd get even dustier, but Rhodes didn't think that was any of his concern. A much-folded road map lay on the seat and there were a few receipts for gasoline on the floor, but there was nothing of any interest to Rhodes.

He walked on up to the house, which looked as if it had been built from used lumber left over from demolished buildings. It was probably sturdy enough, but it wasn't very attractive. It didn't appear to have been painted since it was built. Although some of the boards had paint on them, it seemed to Rhodes that the paint had been put on the boards a long time ago, when they were part of some other structure. He counted at least three different shades of white. On all the planks that he could see, the paint was old and flaking.

The dry, dusty leaves rattled in the trees, and a fresh breeze whisked up the sand in the yard and whirled it into the air. It even dried the sweat on Rhodes's face.

Rhodes looked to the north. The sky was a deep blue, and he thought he saw a flicker of lightning high up in the clouds. The wind was moving on the water of the lake, making little waves that rippled in the sun. A couple of bass boats sat out on the water, and Rhodes could see one of the fishermen casting a lure toward an old rotten tree that was sticking out of the shallow water.

It had been a long time since Rhodes had been fishing, too long, and he wished he could go more often. The bass were supposed to bite just before a front came in, he thought. Or was it just after a front had gone through? Rhodes wasn't sure, not that it mattered. He didn't have time for fishing at the moment. He had other things on his mind.

He walked around to the back of the house. There was a little pier built out from the former shoreline, and normally it would have extended out over the water of the lake. Now it just extended out over the mudflat where the lake had been. There was a snapping-turtle shell lying empty on the former lake floor not far from the pier, as if the turtle had decided for reasons of his own to leave home for good. Rhodes could see a few muddy bottles and aluminum cans sticking out of the mud.

Linda Fenton was sitting on the end of the pier, looking out at the lake. Rhodes climbed the steps to the top of the pier and walked out to join her.

She didn't turn around, but he hadn't tried to sneak up on her. He knew she'd heard him coming. He stood there for a while, waiting for her to acknowledge him. When she didn't, he said, "I didn't think you'd be here."

She didn't turn. She continued to gaze out at the diminished lake. There was nothing there to see except the two bass boats that Rhodes had noticed earlier. The fishermen didn't seem to have had much luck, and the boats were moving away across the water. Rhodes heard the distant buzz of the outboard motors and saw the water turn white and foam in the boats' wakes.

"I didn't think I'd be here, either," Linda said.

"But I started thinking about where I'd go, you know? It turned out that there wasn't anywhere."

"You must have a place."

"I rent a room. That's not really a place. I didn't want to go there."

"I would have found you if you'd gone there and stayed."

"Yeah. I knew that. And I decided I didn't want to run. What's the use, you know?"

Rhodes eased himself down on the end of the dock beside her, careful not to twist in a way that would affect his side. He let his legs dangle off the end of the pier.

"Why did you hit me?" he asked. "I wasn't going to do anything to you."

"I figured that out later. But you were asking too many questions, and I was getting tired of answering."

"I didn't get around to the main one."

"You were working up to it, though. Just because a girl burns a place down doesn't mean she's a killer."

"You were right there near where Grat Bilson died," Rhodes said, "working at that fireworks stand. And when I started talking about Bilson last night, you whacked me with the ashtray. That seems like the reaction of somebody who might be guilty."

"I'm sorry I hit you," Linda told him. "I wish I hadn't done it. I know you can lock me up for it."

241

Rhodes wondered whether she was sorry because he could lock her up or because she felt bad about what she'd done. He didn't think he'd ask.

"Thanks for the apology," he said. "But we still have to talk about Bilson."

"You can talk all you want to. I didn't kill him. I told you why I hit you, and killing somebody didn't have anything to do with it."

"Beaman owned the fireworks stand. He must have told you that Bilson was staying out at that house."

"No, he didn't. I don't even think Jay knew it. We didn't have any reason to kill that man."

"He was trying to find evidence that Jay had accepted a bribe, and he'd already told a newspaper reporter about you. He was determined to cause trouble because Jay had been fooling around with his wife."

"So?"

"So those seem like pretty good reasons to get into an argument with a man. And arguments have a way of getting out of hand." Rhodes touched the back of his head. The knot was hard but tender. "You might even hit someone with an ashtray, or a whiskey bottle if it was handy."

The wind was blowing more strongly now, and it pushed a strand of Linda's hair into her mouth. She moved it aside and tried to put it back in place, but the wind gave her trouble. After a while she gave it up.

"I didn't argue with anybody, and I don't know who did. I just know it wasn't Jay. Okay, so I hit you with that ashtray. That doesn't mean I hit anybody else. I never even saw that Bilson guy."

Rhodes found himself believing her again. He was either getting really gullible, or she was telling the truth. He wished he could make up his mind about which was the case.

From somewhere in the north there was a low grumble of thunder. Rhodes looked up at the sky and saw that it had grown darker and that clouds were moving in, throwing fast-moving shadows on the lake. There was a smell of dampness on the wind.

"Looks like we might finally get some rain," Rhodes said.

"Jay was feeling pretty good about things," Linda said, as if she hadn't heard him. "He told me not long ago that his luck was about to change, you know? He said it was about time he got a break."

"What kind of break?"

"He didn't say, but it had something to do with the hypocrites he had to work with."

"The commissioners?"

"Whatever. He was thinking maybe he could get the fireworks stands to pay off better, the way they had been."

"I thought nobody knew he owned them."

"Nobody did. What I mean was that people like you and some of the other commissioners were making it harder and harder for him to keep them going. He wasn't selling near as many fireworks as he used to, and he needed some way to make more money."

"And he'd found it?"

"I guess so," Linda said. "He didn't tell me what it was, though. All he said was that he and Bilson — is that his name?"

"That's it," Rhodes said.

"Funny name, if you ask me. Anyway, he and Bilson were going to have a little talk, and that Bilson wasn't going to be bothering him anymore. So you can see that he didn't have any reason to kill him."

Once again Rhodes found himself believing her. Although he still remembered getting hit by the ashtray. But what if Beaman had gone to have that little talk with Grat and wound up killing him? It could easily have happened that way.

"I think you might be telling the truth," Rhodes said. "At least as far as you know it. But I have to take you in anyway. You shouldn't have hit me like that."

Linda nodded. "I knew it was a stupid mistake as soon as I did it."

"If you realized it, you should have stayed there. Maybe we could have worked something out."

"Yeah. I thought of that, too, but it was too late by then. I'd already aired up those tires and taken off. I got scared, you know? But I'm not

244

going to run this time. You can take me to jail if you have to."

"All right," Rhodes said.

He managed to stand up without looking too clumsy. He could remember the time when standing up from that position would have been easy. It hadn't been so very long ago, either, or so he told himself.

"Let's go," he said offering a hand to Linda.

She took his hand and stood up a lot more gracefully than he had. As they started walking back down the pier, the first raindrops began to fall.

31

By the time they got to the pickup it was raining hard. The big drops splattered in the sand and rattled off the hood of the truck. Rhodes's shirt was wet through, and his hair was plastered to his head. Linda Fenton looked equally bedraggled.

Rhodes couldn't spare a deputy to come to the lake and drive the pickup back to town, so he decided to take a chance on Linda.

"I'm going to let you follow me," he said. "If we stick to the sandy roads, we should be able to get back to the pavement without getting stuck, but we'll have to go slow."

"What if I run away?"

"I'll have to trust you."

"Right," Linda said.

She got into the truck and rolled up the window while Rhodes ran to the county car. By the time he got there, he was thoroughly soaked, and his shoes were heavy with the wet sand that clung to them. He didn't bother to try cleaning them off. The mud from Wednesday's little adventure was still all over the floor, so Rhodes figured a little more dirt wouldn't matter. He jumped into the car and slammed the door.

Somebody, probably Rhodes himself, would have to clean the car later.

He got from the yard to the road without any difficulty and drove slowly through the increasingly heavy rain. For a couple of minutes it seemed as if the car's wipers were just smearing mud across the windshield, but eventually the dust that had settled on the car earlier was cleaned off and Rhodes could see fairly well.

It had gotten quite dark, so he turned on the lights. Then he glanced into the rearview mirror to see if Linda was actually following him. She was. Rhodes could see the pickup's headlights only a few yards back.

A bright flash of lightning lit up the trees, and a blast of thunder shook their leaves. Rhodes kept driving slowly, hoping for the best. When he came to a part of the road that was more clay than sand, he knew he was in trouble. If he let the wheels drift to one side or the other, he'd slide right off the road into the ditch beside it. And if that happened, he'd be stranded out there for hours. He slowed down even more and didn't relax until he got back safely to the sand. Linda Fenton stayed right behind him.

Just before they came to a paved county road, they crossed a little wooden bridge over what only a few minutes before had been a very dry creek bed. Now, there was water foaming swiftly under the bridge, carrying sticks and dead leaves along with it.

When he reached the pavement, Rhodes

flexed his fingers. He'd been gripping the steering wheel tightly, as if that would help him drive. Now that there was no danger of getting stuck in the mud, he could relax and enjoy the rain. Water was rushing over the road, but he wouldn't have any trouble getting back to town, and it seemed that Linda Fenton was going to come along without causing him any difficulty.

Then he noticed that the headlights he'd been watching in the mirror were no longer there.

The first thing Rhodes decided as he made a U-turn, water hissing under his tires, was that if Linda Fenton got away, he'd never admit to anyone that he'd trusted her.

He especially wouldn't admit it to Ivy.

Getting hit in the head with the ashtray was bad enough, but this was humiliating. How many times did someone have to fool him before he learned his lesson?

He had gone less than a quarter of a mile when he saw the pickup parked on the opposite side of the road. He made another U-turn and pulled up beside it. Linda Fenton was sitting in the driver's seat, but when she saw Rhodes, she opened the door and got out. Then she got into the county car with Rhodes.

"This is the first time I was ever in the front seat of one of these things," she said.

"What happened to the pickup?"

"I don't know. It just stalled out. Something must've gotten wet."

"I thought you'd decided you didn't want to go to jail."

"Yeah, well, I don't, you know? But like I told you, I don't have anyplace else to go. Maybe you can give me some dry clothes."

"They won't be very fashionable," Rhodes said.

"Like I'd care."

"We'll see what we can do."

"This rain's gonna really green things up," Hack said after Linda Fenton was locked in a cell. "The drought might not be over, but this is a big improvement."

"We need more than just one rain," Rhodes said. "We need about a week of this."

After bringing Linda Fenton to the jail, he'd gone home and gotten into dry clothes himself. Going home to change was getting to be a habit, he thought.

"Maybe the rain'll put some water in the lakes and the stock tanks," Lawton said. "Too bad it didn't happen a couple of days ago. Then we coulda had the fireworks on the Fourth."

"I've had enough fireworks for a while," Rhodes said.

"Yeah, but we didn't get to see them," Hack said. "I'd have paid a pretty penny for that show."

"It wouldn't have been worth it," Rhodes said. "It was during the day. The fireworks didn't really show up too well. Not from where I saw them."

"Well, now you got the two women who shot 'em off locked up in the jail," Hack said. "Question is, which one of 'em killed Grat?"

"I'm not sure either one of them did," Rhodes said. "But both of them assaulted me."

"Seems like you get assaulted a lot. Must be the way you treat people."

"I thought I always treated everybody just fine."

"Humpf," Hack said.

Lawton didn't say anything, but from the look on his face, Rhodes could see that he felt pretty much the way Hack did.

"Is there anything you two would like to know that I haven't told you?" he asked, wondering what information they thought he was holding back this time.

"Might be," Hack said.

"What?" Rhodes asked.

He couldn't think of what they could be talking about. As far as he knew, he'd filled them in on just about everything.

"About how you're the rib-eatin' champion of Blacklin County," Lawton said.

As was often the case, Rhodes was completely in the dark, though he hated to admit it, mainly because he knew they were indulging in their favorite pastime: baiting him.

He didn't see any way out of the situation, however, not unless he confessed his ignorance. So he said, "I don't know what you mean."

"We mean you're the big winner," Hack said.

" 'Course people are sayin' you had to kill your competition, and they're not sure that's fair."

"I didn't kill anybody. And I still don't know what you're talking about."

"You must not've heard the radio today," Lawton said. "Seems like you've been announced as the rib-eatin' champ of the whole dang county. They didn't make a big deal out of it, but I guess they didn't figger that'd be in good taste. At the same time, though, they must've wanted somebody to win. Couldn't let something like a dead man stand in the way of givin' out the award. So you won."

"That's ridiculous," Rhodes said.

"Sure is," Hack agreed. "But ridiculous or not, you have to defend your championship next year."

"I don't think so."

"You're the people's choice," Lawton said. "Doesn't make any difference what you think. You gotta play by the rules. The champ has to defend his title."

"It makes a difference to me what I think. I'm not going to enter again. I just did it this time to get a rise out of Beaman."

"You sure got one, all right," Hack said.

Rhodes decided not to pursue the conversation any further. He put on his reading glasses and started to work on his arrest reports, but he hadn't gotten very far when the telephone rang. It was Jennifer Loam, and she wanted to speak to Rhodes.

"Want me to tell her that you're in a sulk and can't talk?" Hack asked.

"I'll talk," Rhodes said, picking up the receiver on his desk.

He greeted the reporter and asked how he could help her.

"I want to know about the latest arrest," she said.

"Which one would that be?"

"Linda Fenton. I understand that she's been arrested."

"Where'd you hear that?"

Rhodes looked around at Hack, who was pretending to be very busy with his computer. Lawton had disappeared.

"Mr. Wilson told me when I called earlier about an interview with Ms. Bilson. He said you were bringing in another prisoner, and I asked him who it was."

"Oh," Rhodes said, turning back to his desk.

"Now I'd like to interview both of them. I could do a long article about the two of them, I think. You know the angle, two women in love with the same man, and now they're sharing the same jail cell."

"I'm not so sure that's a good idea. And they're not sharing the same cell. Maybe you could do something later. I'll think about it."

"What are they charged with?"

"Assault, among other things."

"And they can't talk to a reporter? That's not constitutional."

"They get a phone call, not a meeting with the press."

"How about an interview with you, then?"

"Me? What about?"

"You're the rib-eating champion of Blacklin County. Or didn't you know that?"

"I heard. But I'm not doing interviews."

"It might be a good idea if you did. You could give your side of the story."

"My side?"

"About how you killed Jay Beaman."

Rhodes counted silently to ten. He said, "I didn't kill anybody."

"That's why you need to do the interview. I'll come by around two o'clock."

Rhodes looked at his watch. It was already after one. He was going to tell Jennifer that he'd be out of the office at two, but she'd already hung up. Rhodes put his own phone down and turned to look at Hack again. Hack was still engrossed by something on the computer screen.

"Hack," Rhodes said.

Hack looked up and said, "Yes, sir."

"You've been talking to reporters."

"No law against that. I didn't tell her a thing she couldn't find out by just coming here and asking. It's all a public record."

He had a point. Rhodes said, "She's coming to interview me about Jay Beaman. I don't plan to be here."

"Where you gonna be?"

"Elsewhere."

"What'm I supposed to tell her?"

"Make something up."

"I don't like lyin'," Hack said.

"Then tell her you don't know where I am. That will be the truth."

"No, it won't. I know where you'll be. You'll be out avoidin' her."

"Tell her that, then."

"You shoulda just told her not to come."

"I was about to," Rhodes said. "She hung up on me."

He was about to leave the jail when the phone rang again. It was Dr. White, who had some news for Rhodes.

"I don't want to talk about it on the phone, though," he said. "Can you come by the office?"

Rhodes, who'd been trying to figure out where to go, said, "I'll be there around two o'clock. Will that be all right?"

"I'll make time for you. I'll let the receptionist know you're expected."

Rhodes hung up and said to Hack, "Now you won't have to lie. You can tell Jennifer Loam that I had to visit the doctor."

"What if she asks me if you're sick?"

"Use your imagination," Rhodes said.

32

The rain was still falling, but it had slowed to a drizzle, which was good for the grass and for everything else. The water would have a better chance to soak into the soil.

Rhodes parked as close as he could get to Dr. White's office. As usual the parking lot was nearly full, and when Rhodes got inside, he saw that the waiting room was full as well. People were sitting around looking miserable, some of them sneezing, some coughing, some just silently enduring whatever their problem was while they read tattered magazines. Young children crawled around on the floor playing with red and blue and yellow plastic blocks while their parents watched. The whole place smelled of the peculiar odor typical of doctors' offices and hospitals.

Rhodes wasn't fond of either hospitals or waiting rooms. They reminded him of illness and suffering. He knew that was wrong, that they should remind him of health and healing, but for some reason he could never make himself think that way.

The only thing he liked in Dr. White's waiting room was the aquarium, to which no one else was paying any attention at all. It was full of guppies as colorful as the plastic blocks, and Rhodes watched the fish drift slowly past the glass sides.

The receptionist, a woman of about forty, beckoned to Rhodes, and he walked over to the window. He looked at the receptionist's name tag. It said that she was Brenda. The room behind her was full of gray metal filing cabinets.

"If you'll come through the door," Brenda told him, "I'll take you to Dr. White's office."

Rhodes went through the door and down the hall past the examining rooms. Brenda let him into the doctor's office and said, "He'll be right with you, as soon as he finishes with his current patient."

Rhodes thanked her, and she closed the door behind her as she left. Rhodes looked around the office. Dr. White was the clean-desk type. There was a black leather chair on casters by the desk, and a wooden chair with a cloth cushion was nearby. Rhodes figured that chair was the one designated for visitors, so he sat in it.

The door opened, and Dr. White came in. Rhodes stood up.

"Keep your seat," Dr. White said. "Sorry to keep you waiting."

"That's okay," Rhodes said, sitting back down. "What kind of news do you have that you couldn't talk about on the phone?"

Dr. White settled into the leather chair and leaned back comfortably.

"Oh, I could talk about it," he said. "I just didn't think it would be a good idea. It's pretty unusual."

"Is it about a crime?"

"It's about Jay Beaman."

"Oh," Rhodes said. He felt the muscles tighten in his shoulders. "Is it good news or bad news?"

"Nothing would be good news for Jay Beaman."

"I'm afraid I didn't really have Jay in mind," Rhodes said. "I was more worried about myself."

"In that case, it's probably good news. You didn't kill Jay Beaman."

Rhodes's muscles relaxed a bit. He'd been worried that Dr. White would tell him that the blow on Beaman's head had been the cause of death.

"He had a heart attack, I guess," Rhodes said.

"You should never guess about these things. That's why you asked me to be careful during the autopsy."

"You're always careful. I know that, and I didn't mean to imply that you weren't. I just wanted to be sure that you didn't overlook any-thing."

"I don't blame you. And you were right to caution me. It's a good thing I was careful. Oth-erwise, I might have thought that Beaman died from colliding with that rock wall. I was there. I saw it happen. It would be a natural conclusion, except that his head was hardly affected."

"So that's not what did it," Rhodes said.

"Correct." Dr. White's manner was grim. "But it wasn't a heart attack, either."

"It wasn't?"

"No. What you said made me stop and think about my methods. We're a small town, and I don't always do as complete a job as I could. Maybe not even as complete as I should, because, as you pointed out, I usually think I know the cause of death, and that can make a man get careless. In Grat Bilson's case, I did check for smoke in the lungs so we'd know whether he died in the fire, of course. But the back of his head was caved in, after all. Checking was the logical thing to do."

Rhodes couldn't quite figure out where the doctor was going with all this, but he didn't want to interrupt.

"Anyway," Dr. White continued, "I didn't want to be careless this time, so I ran a lot of tests that I wouldn't ordinarily fool with. It's a good thing I did, too, or I'd have missed it completely."

Rhodes still didn't understand what Dr. White was getting at. He said, "Missed what?"

"The cause of death. It was obvious, but only if I ran the tests."

"But it wasn't a heart attack?"

"No."

"Stroke? Aneurysm?"

"No and no. It wasn't anything in the usual way of things. I'd never seen anything like it."

"What, then?" Rhodes asked.

"Poison," Dr. White said. "Jay Beaman was poisoned."

Rhodes couldn't think of anything to say. He just sat there, looking at Dr. White.

"I'm surprised he was able to fight you for as long as he did," the doctor continued. "But then he had only a tiny dose. It was ingested. The poison used is so deadly that it will kill on contact with the skin. It doesn't take much to kill someone using that method, but ingestion will work just as quickly. Believe me, it's powerful stuff."

"I believe you," Rhodes said. "What is it?"

"Dichlorovinyl dimethyl phosphate. DVDP for short. In almost its purest form. It's easy to make it if you know how. You could mix it up on your back porch if you wanted to, but you'd have to be very, very careful. It's a good thing not many people want to do it, or we'd have a lot more dead people around."

Rhodes hadn't thought Dr. White was so cynical.

"You think people would go around poisoning everybody in the county?" he asked.

"No. Of course not. People would kill themselves mixing it up. It's extremely toxic."

"What are the ingredients?"

Dr. White told him, and Rhodes thought things over for a few seconds. Then he said, "You're sure that's what killed Jay Beaman."

"No question about it. You're officially off the hook if that's what's worrying you."

"It's not that," Rhodes said. He looked at his watch. It was five minutes after two o'clock. "Mind if I use your telephone?"

"Help yourself. Punch nine for an outside line."

Rhodes called the jail and got Hack on the line.

"Is Jennifer Loam still there?"

"She sure is, Sheriff. I was just explaining to her how you took sick all of a sudden and had to rush off to the doctor's office. I guess that's where you are right now."

"As a matter of fact, I am," Rhodes said. "Put Jennifer on the phone."

Rhodes heard mumbling in the background, and then the reporter said, "Yes, Sheriff?"

"I've just been talking to Dr. White," Rhodes said. "I want you to wait there at the jail for me. I'll be there in five minutes."

"Are you going to give me a story?"

"No," Rhodes said. "You're going to give me one."

33

When Rhodes got back to the jail, it had stopped raining completely. The clouds were gone, the sun was shining, and there appeared to be steam rising from the sidewalk. Rhodes knew it wasn't really steam, but it made him feel uncomfortable just the same. Because of the high humidity, it seemed much hotter than it had even on the hottest of the dry days. By the time Rhodes had walked from his air-conditioned car to the door of the jail, his shirt was sticking to his back as if he'd been rained on again.

As soon as he got inside, Rhodes asked Lawton if there was a vacant cell away from the ones holding prisoners.

"We got one like that," Lawton said.

"Good," Rhodes said. "Show me where it is. Come on, Ms. Loam."

They followed Lawton, who opened the cell. Rhodes told Lawton to go on back to the office and sit with Hack. As soon as Lawton had left, Rhodes asked Jennifer to go inside the cell and sit on the cot while he checked the neighboring cells to make sure that they were indeed empty.

"This is a terrible place," Jennifer said when Rhodes returned. She looked around at the stone walls, the barely adequate sanitary facilities, and the barred windows. "I'm not sure I want to sit on that cot."

"It's clean," Rhodes said. "Courtesy of Blacklin County."

"I think I'd prefer to stand anyway. It's awfully hot in here, isn't it?"

"That's what the prisoners think," Rhodes said. "Hack believes they'll file a lawsuit."

"That would be a good story," Jennifer said.

Rhodes could see why she'd think so, but he didn't want to talk about that. She said, "Why don't you tell me what we're doing here?"

"It was the most private place I could think of that we could get to quickly. I want you to tell me a few things, and I don't want any evasive answers."

"I'm not sure what you mean."

"I think you do. You were working on your big story, and you were talking to Grat Bilson a lot. You even knew about a so-called bribe that Jay Beaman was supposed to have taken. I think you knew more about the commissioners than you told me."

Jennifer looked down at the cell floor, which was no more attractive than the rest of the place.

"Not a lot," she said after a few seconds had gone by.

"A little, then. You shouldn't have held anything back. This is a murder investigation. You'll have to tell me what you know."

"No, I don't. I don't have to tell you anything. You guessed who my source was, but I didn't even have to confirm that."

"Look," Rhodes said, with more patience than he was feeling, "the only reason you're alive now is that phone call you got about me, the one telling you I was using inmates to paint my house."

"Are you trying to scare me?"

"No. I'm just trying to impress you with how important this is."

"What does that phone call have to do with anything?"

"When did you get the call?" Rhodes asked.

"I don't like for people to answer a question with a question," Jennifer said.

"I wasn't answering you. I was asking you a different question. Now tell me. When did you get that call?"

Jennifer opened her purse and got out her notebook. She flipped through a few pages, then stopped.

"Well?" Rhodes said.

"July second, not long before I called you."

"There's the problem," Rhodes said. "When you got that call, your source was already dead."

"Oh," Jennifer said. "But if Mr. Bilson was dead, who called me?"

"Someone else, someone who wanted to discredit your story. It's like I said when you told me about the call. If that part of your story is wrong, then why should anyone believe the rest of it? You couldn't print the story. Your source was unreliable."

"But the person who called sounded like Mr. Bilson."

"Did you take the call on your cell phone?"

"Yes."

"Sometimes the reception can break up," Rhodes said. "Was it like that?"

"It could have been. I don't remember."

Rhodes thought that it had. Or that the breaking up had been faked.

"Maybe he was scared to kill you," Rhodes said. "Your death would have been awfully hard to explain. It would have made someone, maybe me, dig even deeper. I might have found out some of the things that you already know. So he decided to discredit your source instead."

"I told you that I don't really know all that much," Jennifer said.

"But you do know something, don't you? Probably something related to what I was accused of. That would make sense. Plant a false story about something similar to what was really going on, and you cast doubt on anyone who accuses you of having done the same thing."

"But who would do that?"

"I think that's pretty obvious."

"The killer?" Jennifer said.

"Right. And he'd kill you, too, if he thought you were a danger to him."

"But why kill Mr. Beaman?"

"Let's talk about what you know, first. To make sure you're really not in any danger."

"I'm not in danger because I don't know that much. Just one little thing."

"It's connected to that bribe, isn't it," Rhodes said.

"Yes. It wasn't a bribe so much as a quid pro quo. That means —"

"I know what that means," Rhodes said. "I might look like an ignorant jerk, but I'm not."

"Sorry."

"Never mind. Bilson thought Jay was doing something for Ralph Oliver, didn't he. Something that involved using county materials or county workers."

Jennifer looked him over. "I guess you're not an ignorant jerk after all."

"Thanks," Rhodes said.

"You don't have to be sarcastic. Anyway, you're right. That's all it was. Mr. Bilson thought that Beaman used county materials and maybe even some workers to help build Ralph Oliver's house. Have you seen that place?"

Rhodes said that he had.

"It's like something out of some old movie."

"I know," Rhodes said. "*Gone with the Wind.*"

"I was thinking of *Hannibal.*"

"That was the Biltmore estate," Rhodes said, feeling his age. His hair was thinning, all right, no doubt about it. For him, *Gone with the Wind* was an old movie; for Jennifer Loam, *Hannibal* was.

"What's the Biltmore estate?" Jennifer asked.

Rhodes wondered what they were teaching in journalism schools these days, but maybe it was just another sign of his age that he knew who the Biltmores were and Jennifer didn't.

"Never mind," Rhodes said. "It doesn't matter. We seem to have drifted off the subject."

"We?"

"All right, I drifted off the subject. What was the subject, by the way?"

"That house of Ralph Oliver's," Jennifer said. "The cost of building a place like that is tremendous, and have you seen that curved driveway?"

Rhodes said that he'd seen it.

"How much would something like that cost? And how much concrete would it take?"

Rhodes didn't know. He asked what that had to do with anything.

"The county has plenty of concrete. Suppose that some of those road contracts bought items that never went into roads. Suppose they went into the building of Mr. Oliver's house and driveway and barn instead."

"Exactly what I was saying. You have the proof?"

"No, but I'm working on it."

"Good," Rhodes told her. "You keep working. If you can get the proof, we'll put him away."

Jennifer seemed to think that was an excellent idea, and she was even happier when Rhodes led her out of the cell and back to the office.

She seemed to be in a hurry to leave and get

back to her story, and Rhodes didn't try to keep her any longer. He'd confirmed his suspicions, and he didn't want Jennifer to know what he was going to do next. If she'd known, she would probably have insisted on going along with him.

As soon as she left the jail, Rhodes told Hack to call for some backup.

"Get Buddy Ferguson," he said, "or Ruth. It doesn't matter. Whoever's the closest."

"That would be Buddy. He's probably somewhere around Milsby about now. It'll take him a while to get there, though. Why do you think you'll need him?"

"I'm going to have a talk with Ralph Oliver, and he might not like what I have to say."

"What're you gonna say?" Hack asked.

"That he killed Jay Beaman," Rhodes said.

34

No one was sitting on the porch of the Olivers' house when Rhodes arrived this time. He parked the county car and got out. The grass was, if anything, even greener than the last time he'd been there, as if it had been fertilized heavily.

Rhodes was about to step up on the porch when he heard something from around behind the house, a soft *whoomp* followed by the solid sound of a tennis ball being hit with a tautly strung racket.

Rhodes walked around the house on the soggy grass and spongy ground. His shirt stuck to his back in the steamy heat. When he got to the back, which was quite a hike, he saw both Olivers on their tennis court, which was painted almost the same color green as the grass.

Julia Oliver was sitting in a director's chair beside the court. She was wearing a white visor, white shorts, white shoes, and a white shirt. She watched as her husband, who was also dressed all in white, tried to return the balls that were being shot to his side of the court by a mechanical ball launcher. The noise the launcher made reminded Rhodes just a little of the sound of the

Roman candles that had been firing over his head only a couple of days earlier.

Rhodes stood quietly until the balls stopped coming out of the machine. Then he walked over beside Julia and said, "Good afternoon."

"Oh, hello, Sheriff," she said. She seemed as cool and dry as the star of a deodorant commercial. "It's nice to see you again. Can I get you something to drink?"

Rhodes didn't think she'd have said it was nice to see him if she had any idea why he was there, much less offered him a drink. He didn't see any lemonade around, so he thought that accepting her offer might give him a chance to talk with her husband.

"I'd like some lemonade if you have it," he said.

"I can mix some up in a jiffy," she said. "I'll get glasses for all of us. I'm sure Ralph will need it."

She got up gracefully and walked away just as her husband came over. He was wiping his face and hair with a thick white towel.

"This is as bad as living on the Gulf Coast," he said. "I hate humidity like this."

Rhodes said that he didn't like it very much either.

Oliver tossed the towel on a chair beside the one his wife had vacated and said, "Did Julia go for something to drink?"

"That's right."

"Good. I need something cold for sure.

What's going on with you, Sheriff? Two visits in two days, that's pretty unusual, considering you've never been here before."

"I came here to talk to you about the murder of Jay Beaman," Rhodes said.

Oliver laughed. He picked up the towel from the chair and wiped his face again, then sat in the chair with the towel across his lap. He looked up at Rhodes and said, "Murder? You're kidding me, right?"

"I'm not kidding you."

"Well, then, talk away. Everybody knows it wasn't murder. It was plain as day that you killed Beaman in self-defense, but if you've been accused of murder, I'll be glad to stand up for you. I was there, and I saw the whole thing. Beaman jumped you, and you just did what you had to do. Him hitting his head on that wall wasn't your fault. It was just an accident."

Oliver would have made a great salesman, Rhodes thought. Or maybe he was a salesman, in a way. He convinced people to do illegal things for him, and that was at least as hard as selling shoes or used cars. Rhodes was also pretty sure that Oliver had been making payments to various commissioners over the years to assure his getting plenty of road contracts. Bribing them, but convincing them that it wasn't a bribe. A man would have to be pretty persuasive to do something like that.

"I didn't kill Jay Beaman," Rhodes said. "That's why I'm here."

"I know you didn't kill him on purpose. I just said that."

Rhodes was getting a little aggravated with Oliver, who wasn't cooperating at all. He was supposed to break down under the sheriff's steely glare and confess to everything. Instead, he wouldn't even admit that anything had happened.

A door closed in the house, and Rhodes looked over to see Julia coming toward them with a pitcher of lemonade and three glasses on a tray. She crossed the grass to the court and set the tray on a little wooden table between the two chairs.

"If you don't mind, Sheriff," she said, "I'll pour Ralph's drink first. I'm sure he's thirsty after that little workout of his."

She poured the lemonade and handed it to Oliver, who took a long swallow.

"That was great," he said. "Julia, if you were called to testify in court, would you say that Sheriff Rhodes killed Jay Beaman in self-defense?"

Julia handed Rhodes a glass of lemonade and said, "I most certainly would. That Jay Beaman was like a wild man. I'm sorry you had to kill him, though, Sheriff. That was a terrible thing."

Rhodes set his glass down on the tray and said, "I didn't kill anyone. I think you did."

Julia's eyes widened. "Me? Me?"

"You," Rhodes said.

She moved jerkily toward her husband's chair.

She bumped the table and knocked the pitcher and two glasses to the grass. They were made of plastic, so they didn't break. One of the glasses bounced off the pitcher and landed on the ice cubes that had spilled out.

Oliver stood up and took his wife in his arms.

"You shouldn't say things like that," he told Rhodes. "You've upset Julia, and that upsets me. You'll have to leave now."

Rhodes wasn't going anywhere. He said, "Sorry to upset you, Julia, but Jay Beaman didn't die when his head hit the wall. According to the autopsy, he was already dead when he fell."

Dr. White hadn't actually said that, but Rhodes was sure he would have if he'd thought of it.

"That's baloney," Oliver said. "His head hit the wall, he died, end of story."

"No," Rhodes said, "that's only the beginning. He didn't die when his head hit the wall. He died when he was poisoned. And you poisoned him."

Julia had started sobbing into Oliver's shoulder.

"You're just making things worse," Oliver told Rhodes. "If you don't leave here on your own, I'll have to make you."

Rhodes didn't move. He said, "You did it with the ribs. That last little plate you put down right by him. Nobody else was anywhere near through eating, so you didn't have to worry about somebody grabbing them."

"You're nuts. Why would I do that?"

"Because he was going to tell all about how you got your house, your driveway, your barn, probably your tennis court here."

"And how was that?"

"By using county materials and county workmen. I might not be able to prove the part about the poison, but I can prove the rest."

Julia started crying harder, and Rhodes figured it was because she knew exactly what her husband had been up to. It would have been almost impossible to keep it secret from her, although Rhodes wasn't sure about the poisoning. She might not have known about that. He'd accused her only to get a reaction from Oliver.

"The materials weren't hard to steal," Rhodes said. "You just had them delivered to a work site and took them from there. Nobody would question it if you took your own stuff. Probably no one even noticed. I don't know how you got the county workmen to do the job, and maybe you didn't. Maybe you just used your own men instead, when they were supposed to be working on a road. And then you let the county pay for the time. That should be pretty easy to prove, too."

Julia pulled away from her husband and, still crying, ran to the house. Rhodes watched her go, then turned back to Oliver.

"Don't blame me for what your wife is going through," Rhodes said. "It's not my fault. It's yours. And it's only going to get worse. Your

273

murder trial is going to be harder on her than it is on you."

"You son of a bitch."

"You should get together with Yvonne Bilson," Rhodes said.

"I never murdered anybody," Oliver said. "You try digging up anything between me and Beaman. Question everybody at his place. I don't care. I'm innocent."

Rhodes was tired of the denials. He was about to tell Oliver to come along with him to the jail when Buddy Ferguson walked around the house.

"What's going on, Sheriff?" Buddy asked. "Need any help with this fella?"

Buddy was thin, puritanical, and devoted to his job. There was nothing he liked better than arresting lawbreakers.

"I don't need any help," Rhodes said. "I'm sure Mr. Oliver will cooperate."

"Like hell I will," Oliver said, swinging his tennis racket and hitting Rhodes in the face with a solidly credible backhand.

Rhodes felt the waffle pattern of the strings as they stung him and impressed themselves on his cheek. He stumbled to the side, stepped on the lemonade pitcher, and fell.

He heard Buddy yell, "Freeze!" and then the shooting started.

35

Rhodes pushed himself up and saw Oliver running a serpentine path toward the barn, slipping and sliding, with mud flying up around his feet.

Buddy was firing his pistol into the air. Rhodes was relieved. He'd thought Buddy was shooting at Oliver.

Apparently, so did Oliver, who was moving pretty well for a middle-aged contractor, Rhodes thought.

"That's enough shooting," Rhodes said, standing up. "I don't think you slowed him down any."

"Nope," Buddy said holstering his pistol, a big .357 magnum, "but he was sure moving along, wasn't he? You want me to go after him?"

"We'll both go," Rhodes said, and they started across the tennis court.

Oliver had a good head start, and he got to the barn by the time Rhodes and Buddy had crossed the court and gotten back onto the lawn. As it turned out, the lawn didn't extend all the way to the barn. Beginning about ten yards from the tennis court, there was an expanse that was mostly weeds and mud. Rhodes thought it was a miracle that Oliver hadn't fallen.

Buddy and Rhodes were about halfway to the

barn when Rhodes heard the sound of a motor starting.

"Come on," he said, and started running.

His feet slipped and slued, but he didn't fall, not even when he got almost to the barn and a large black pickup came roaring out at him.

The truck had an extended cab and four doors. It couldn't get much traction on the mud after leaving the barn, and the back wheels spun freely, throwing up a geyser of mud behind the truck, which moved slowly in Rhodes's direction.

Rhodes dodged out of the way, and when the truck passed him, he stepped into the mudbath that was being flung up behind it and grabbed hold of the tailgate. He had to run to keep up with the pickup, and mud splattered all over him, slapping wetly into his clothes and even his face. But he kept his grip on the tailgate until he could get a foot on the bumper and pull himself into the truck bed.

He was getting used to being covered with mud, but he was getting tired of having to clean the bathroom. Oliver would have to pay for that, Rhodes told himself. He moved along the bed until he got to the back window of the cab. Even if it had opened, which it didn't, Rhodes was sure he couldn't have crawled through it. In spite of all the tofu cheese he'd eaten, he just wasn't slender enough. He thought about smashing the window with his pistol butt, but that didn't seem like such a good idea. There was no telling what Oliver would do.

Standing up, Rhodes put his hands on top of the cab and looked to see where they were heading. The truck had passed by Buddy and was almost back to the house, and its tires were digging deep ruts through Oliver's beautifully kept lawn. He didn't seem to care. Rhodes wondered if the county had been unwittingly paying for the upkeep of the yard, and if so, for how long.

Oliver must have thought that he'd left Rhodes and Buddy behind because he stopped the truck at the back of the house and jumped out.

"Stop right there," Rhodes said, pulling his pistol and bracing his arms on top of the cab.

Oliver looked back in surprise, said, "You son of a bitch" again, and ran inside the house.

Rhodes didn't shoot. He put his gun away and climbed out of the truck bed. Only a year or so ago, he would have jumped out, but he wasn't as limber and flexible as he once had been.

Buddy came running across the tennis court.

"Why didn't you shoot him?" Buddy asked.

"Same reason you didn't," Rhodes said. "He's unarmed, and he deserves a trial."

"What for, if you don't mind my asking?"

"He killed Jay Beaman."

"Dang. I thought *you* killed Jay."

Rhodes was getting tired of hearing that. He said, "I didn't kill anybody. Jay didn't die because of our fight. He was poisoned."

"Well, I'll be a blue-nosed gopher."

Rhodes thought that Buddy watched too many old Gabby Hayes westerns on television. He said, "Go around front and be sure he doesn't leave that way. I'll go in the back."

"You be careful."

"Don't worry," Rhodes said. "I will."

The inside of the house was pleasantly cool after all the humidity outdoors, and Rhodes could feel the sweat drying on his body almost immediately.

The kitchen, where Rhodes found himself, wasn't just cool. It was spotlessly clean, and Rhodes almost felt guilty about the fact that he was depositing mud on everything he touched and everywhere he stepped.

He would have felt even guiltier if there hadn't been muddy footprints on the tile floor already, put there by Oliver as he'd passed through.

So the mud, Rhodes told himself, was all Oliver's fault. If Oliver had just cooperated, the house would have stayed clean.

Positioning himself at the side of the stairs so that he couldn't be seen from the second floor, Rhodes called out to Oliver to come down.

There was no reply, not that Rhodes had been expecting one. He decided that he'd have to go up.

Rhodes climbed to the top, pausing when he got there.

"Oliver?" he said. "You might as well come on out. We've got the house surrounded."

Maybe, he thought, *I'm the one who's been watching too many old westerns on TV.*

Oliver stepped out of one of the rooms at the end of the hallway. He was still dressed in his whites, though they were somewhat muddy now. And he was no longer holding his tennis racket.

He was holding instead a 12-gauge automatic shotgun, and he was pointing it right at Rhodes.

"Back off, Sheriff," he said. "I'm going down those stairs, and Julia's going with me."

Julia was standing behind him, looking as frightened as anyone Rhodes had ever seen, her eyes still red from crying, though now she was silent.

"You don't want to get into a shooting match with me," Rhodes said. "I might hit Julia."

As soon as he said it, Julia gave a little screech and disappeared back into the room where she'd been hiding.

"Now you won't hit her," Oliver said, not looking to see where she'd gone.

"I might hit you, though," Rhodes said.

"I don't think so. After the buckshot takes you apart, there won't be enough left of you to pull the trigger of that pistol."

Rhodes knew that Oliver wasn't exaggerating. A good load of double-ought buckshot could make a pretty big mess of a person, especially at close range, and Oliver looked crazy enough to shoot. Things had been going along pretty well until Buddy walked up, Rhodes thought, and then Oliver had panicked. Suddenly the prospect of actually going to jail must have seemed all too real, and now Oliver had become desperate.

"Why don't you just put the pistol down on the floor and get out of the way," Oliver said. "I can pick it up as I leave, and you won't get hurt."

"You can't leave," Rhodes said. "My deputies are outside waiting for you."

"There's only one deputy out there. You know it, and I know it. He can't watch the front and the back at the same time, so I'll find a way to get by him. Now put the gun down before I have to shoot you."

Rhodes tried to decide just how desperate Oliver was. He'd already killed one man, and he might think he didn't have anything to lose by killing another.

"Killing a police officer while he's performing his duty is a capital offense," Rhodes said. "You might get off with life for killing Beaman."

"I don't much care," Oliver said.

Rhodes could see that he was sweating in spite of the air-conditioning. That wasn't a good sign, but Rhodes wasn't going to step aside. He got ready to jump, just in case Oliver made up his mind to fire. It was one thing to poison somebody. It was something else again to shoot a man who was looking you in the eye, or so Rhodes told himself. And he wondered how much good it would do him to jump. Not much, if the buckshot didn't come out of the barrel in a tight pattern. If it spread fast, it could clear the entire hallway.

"All right," Oliver said. "You brought this on yourself."

Oliver's eyes narrowed, Rhodes jumped, and Oliver pulled the trigger.

36

The shotgun blast boomed off the walls, and the buckshot tore a gigantic hole in the ceiling of the hallway.

The gun was pointing upward because Julia Oliver had come out of hiding and shoved her husband hard in the back. And not a moment too soon, as far as Rhodes was concerned.

Rhodes bounced off the wall, and when Oliver brought the weapon back down level, Rhodes was on him. He grabbed the barrel of the gun and jerked it out of Oliver's hands.

There was a pop, and Oliver screamed. Rhodes thought that Oliver's finger had caught in the trigger guard and gotten broken. Rhodes didn't much care. His ears were ringing again, and he was beginning to think he'd have to start wearing ear protection as a normal part of his daily attire.

He thanked Julia for her help, but she was crying and probably didn't hear, not if the shotgun blast had affected her in the same way it had affected Rhodes.

Oliver was bent over, holding his hands together between his thighs and moaning. Rhodes prodded him in the back with the shotgun and told him to go downstairs.

"You son of a bitch," Oliver wailed. His voice sounded hollow and distant. "You broke my goddamned finger!"

"I'm sorry about that," Rhodes lied. "But you were resisting arrest. Now let's go down."

Oliver went, stopping now and then to glare over his shoulder at Rhodes.

When they got to the bottom of the stairs, Buddy was standing there, his pistol trained on Oliver, who was still holding his hand and whimpering.

"I heard a gun go off," Buddy said.

"Mr. Oliver tried to shoot me," Rhodes said, holding up the shotgun. "He missed."

"I can see that. But if mud was blood, you'd be a dead man."

"Go upstairs and see about Mrs. Oliver. Try to get her to call a friend if she hasn't already done it, somebody to come and stay with her for a while."

"You taking this guy to jail?"

"Yes."

"Why's he all bent over like that?"

"I think he broke his finger."

"Too bad," Buddy said, but he was smiling and Rhodes could tell he didn't mean it.

After Oliver was booked and locked up, Hack called Dr. White and asked him to come and have a look at Oliver's finger. Just as he hung up the phone, Buddy came through the front door of the jail. He told Rhodes that Mrs. Oliver had called someone, and when she'd arrived, Buddy had left.

"Is Mrs. Oliver still upset?" Rhodes asked.

"I don't think so. Seemed more relieved than anything. I wouldn't be surprised if she was happy to have her husband behind bars."

"You want me to call that reporter now?" Hack asked Rhodes. "She can write about how you've cracked another big case."

"I don't think you need to call anybody just yet," Rhodes said.

"She'll be mighty upset if you don't let her know."

"I'll let her know when I'm ready," Rhodes said. "I'm going home to clean up now."

"Gotta admit that you could use it," Hack said. "You get any more mud on you, you can start your own pig sty."

"I don't mind the mud," Rhodes said. "It's the cleanup I don't like."

"That's what a sheriff's job is," Buddy said. "Cleaning up. You go out and clean up the trash and bring it here."

"That's not what I meant," Rhodes said. "But sometimes I don't like that either."

It was almost five o'clock when Rhodes finished bathing, changing clothes, and cleaning the bathroom one more time. He could have done what he had to do with the mud still on him, but he knew he'd feel better about things if he was clean. Not that he was going to feel good about any part of it, clean or not. He usually liked his job, but he didn't like it very much at the moment.

He drove out to the precinct barn. Mrs. Wilkie was cleaning off her desk and getting ready to leave when he walked in.

"Why, hello, Sheriff," she said. "Wasn't that a nice rain we got today?"

Rhodes was glad she hadn't asked if it was hot enough for him. He agreed that the rain had been nice and asked if Allen was in.

"I think he might be outside in the barn. You can just go on through his office if you want to. I'm sure he wouldn't mind."

Rhodes thanked her and walked through Allen's office and out the door that led to the barn. Allen was standing by a dump truck talking to someone. When he saw Rhodes, he waved, said something to the man by the truck, and then walked over to join Rhodes, who was looking up at the roof.

"Good little rain we got this morning," Allen said. "What are you looking at up there?"

"Those pest strips," Rhodes said, pointing. "I thought those things were illegal."

"They've been hanging up there for years," Allen said. "We just never got around to taking them down."

"I guess you probably even have some still in the original packages."

Something changed in Allen's eyes. Rhodes

wouldn't have noticed if he hadn't been looking for it. He was sorry to see it, however.

"I don't think we have any around," Allen said. "What's this all about, anyway?"

"You can make poison with those things. Did you know that?"

Allen looked away, first up at the strips that hung from the ceiling and then off to one side.

"Poison?" Allen said. "No. I didn't know that. Who cares?"

"Jay Beaman, for one," Rhodes said. He felt tired. Maybe it was all the mud. "What I can't figure out is how you got mixed up in all this. I thought it was Beaman, but it was you all along."

"I don't know what you're talking about," Allen said, but Rhodes could tell that he knew, all right.

"I should've figured it out when I saw the way Beaman lived," Rhodes said. "He had an old house that needed a lot of work. His lake house was even worse. It looked like something he might've built himself on weekends. But your house, well, that's a little different."

"You know why my house is big. I have a lot of kids."

"You sure do. Which makes me wonder how you can afford to keep the place up like you do. It looks a lot better than the one Beaman lived in. And that paved road of yours should have been the tip-off. You and Oliver were working together, weren't you?"

Allen looked as if he might be sick. He said, "What's Oliver got to do with anything?"

"He's the one who poisoned Beaman. You knew about it, though, didn't you?"

"Beaman? I thought he hit his head during that fight with you."

"No, you didn't think that. You helped make the poison that killed him, or maybe you made it by yourself. I don't know, but I think you'll tell me. Killing Beaman might have been Oliver's idea, but you were in on it. Oliver's already in jail, by the way. I'm sure he'll start talking before long, so you might as well get your side of the story told first. Sometimes it's better that way."

"I don't have a side," Allen said. "I don't have a story. Look, Dan, you've known me since we were kids. You know I wouldn't do something crazy like that."

Rhodes was sorry that he had to hear the pleading note in his old friend's voice. He was even sorrier that he knew Allen was guilty.

"There was a time I wouldn't have thought you'd do it," Rhodes said. "But people change, I guess. Here's what I think happened. I think Grat Bilson, while he was snooping around and trying to dig up some dirt on Beaman, found something on you instead. He didn't feel about you the way he felt about Beaman, so maybe he called you up and asked you to talk things over with him. Maybe he even thought you could help him get Beaman, and if you could, well, he'd just forget what he knew about you. But things didn't work out, you argued, and you hit him with a whiskey bottle that happened to be sitting around. You probably didn't mean to kill him. It was an accident. I know that."

Allen didn't say anything. The man that Allen had been talking to earlier left the barn, waving in Allen's direction as he did. Allen didn't wave back. Rhodes didn't think Allen even saw the other man leave.

"You didn't know what to do," Rhodes went on, "so you thought it would be a good idea to make people think Grat had died in a fire. You doused him with whiskey and gasoline and set the fire. I never did find the gas can. I figure you put it in the back of your truck and forgot about it."

Allen looked over his shoulder as if his truck were parked right there.

"The can's still there, huh?" Rhodes said. "Well, don't worry too much about that. We probably can't prove it was Grat's in the first place, unless he had his name on it. But we have your fingerprints on the whiskey bottle."

Rhodes was only guessing about the fingerprints, since the report hadn't come back. But Allen didn't know that.

"I don't know how Beaman got onto you," Rhodes said. "But I'd bet he figured it out because of things Grat was saying and that Jennifer Loam talked to him about. Beaman knew that if there was any bribing going on, he wasn't getting his share, and he knew he wasn't furnishing any county help to work on Oliver's house. He thought maybe it was you, and Grat might have confirmed it to him. The next election, you'd have been in big trouble, and Beaman wouldn't have had to worry about his fireworks stands anymore."

"Fireworks stands?"

"He owned every one of them in the county," Rhodes said. "That's why he was going to let the world know about you. So he could get you off his case. Bilson must have told you that he knew about you and Oliver, and I think Beaman suspected that you killed Bilson. So you went to Oliver, and the two of you decided to get rid of Beaman. Oliver might have put the poison on the ribs, but you're the one who told him how to make it. You had the strips right here."

"I have kids in college," Allen said. "I have five more who want to go. I needed money, and Oliver made it seem like working with him wasn't really a bad thing to do."

"It would've been tough for you to send your kids to college without Oliver's money, but you could've managed it somehow. It's going to be a lot tougher on them now."

Allen's shoulders sagged. He said, "Ralph and I didn't think anybody would check for the poison. We thought everyone would just think it was a heart attack."

"That might have worked," Rhodes said. "But

it was a long chance. It got even longer when we had to do the autopsy."

"What's my wife going to think? What about my kids?"

"I don't know," Rhodes said. "I just don't know."

The front that had brought the rain passed on through. It took the humidity with it, leaving the air dry and the sky clear. It was a long time until fall, and there would be more days to come when the temperature climbed past one hundred degrees, but the hot, dry night didn't feel nearly as oppressive as the moisture-laden afternoon.

When Rhodes got home after a long interview with Jennifer Loam, he saw fireflies sparkling in the grass in the backyard. Speedo was sitting on his haunches, watching Yancey, who was trying to catch fireflies. He wasn't having much luck. Either they would flicker out and he would lose them or they would fly up over his head, causing him to bounce up on his hind legs, yipping and pawing at the empty air where they had just been.

The dog's antics cheered Rhodes up a little. He was feeling as bad about arresting a man as he'd ever felt before, which was a shame. There was no reason to feel bad. James Allen was guilty, after all. But Rhodes had never had to jail a friend before, a man he'd known for more years than he liked to think about. And he felt sorry for Allen's family. It would take them a long time to recover from what Allen had done, if they ever did. Allen should have thought of that, of course, but Rhodes was pretty sure most people never really considered the consequences of their actions. They just did what they thought would benefit them most at the time.

Ivy was standing on the porch, watching the dogs and waiting for Rhodes. He wasn't looking forward to telling her about Allen, but he knew she'd want to know.

He walked on over to the porch and looked up at her.

"Hot enough for you?" he said.

ABOUT THE AUTHOR

Bill Crider lives with his wife, Judy, in Alvin, Texas, where he serves as chair of the Division of English and Fine Arts at Alvin Community College. *Red, White, and Blue Murder* is his thirteenth novel about the likable lawman Dan Rhodes. In addition to the Rhodes novels, Crider is the author of a series about Sally Good, chair of the English Department in a community college that has a lot in common with the one in Alvin, if far fewer homicides.